The Traitor

GOLDEN MOUNTAIN
CHRONICLES: 1885

Also by
Laurence Yep

Golden Mountain Chronicles

*The extraordinary intergenerational story of the Young family
from Three Willows Village, Kwangtung province,
China, and their lives in the Land of the
Golden Mountain—America.*

The Serpent's Children (1849)

Mountain Light (1855)

Dragon's Gate (1867)
A Newbery Honor Book

The Traitor (1885)

Dragonwings (1903)
A Newbery Honor Book

The Red Warrior (1939)
Coming soon

Child of the Owl (1965)

Sea Glass (1970)

Thief of Hearts (1995)

Dragon of the Lost Sea Fantasies

Dragon of the Lost Sea

Dragon Steel

Dragon Cauldron

Dragon War

When the Circus Came to Town
The Dragon Prince
Dream Soul
The Imp That Ate My Homework
The Magic Paintbrush
The Rainbow People
The Star Fisher

Chinatown Mysteries
The Case of the Goblin Pearls
The Case of the Lion Dance
The Case of the Firecrackers

Edited by Laurence Yep
American Dragons
Twenty-Five Asian American Voices

The Traitor

GOLDEN MOUNTAIN
CHRONICLES: 1885

HarperCollins*Publishers*

The Traitor

www.harperchildrens.com

Library of Congress Cataloging-in-Publication Data

Yep, Laurence.
 The Traitor : Golden Mountain chronicles, 1885 / Laurence Yep.
 p. cm.
 Summary: In 1885, a lonely illegitimate American boy and a lonely Chinese American boy develop an unlikely friendship in the midst of prejudices and racial tension in their coal mining town of Rock Springs, Wyoming.
 ISBN 0-06-027522-7 — ISBN 0-06-027523-5 (lib. bdg.)
 [1. Prejudices—Fiction. 2. Friendship—Fiction. 3. Chinese Americans—Fiction. 4. Illegitimate children—Fiction. 5. Coal mines and mining—Fiction. 6. Rock Springs Massacre, Rock Springs, Wyo., 1885—Fiction. 7. West (U.S.)—History—19th century—Fiction.] I. Title.
PZ7.Y44 Tr 2003   2002022534
[Fic]—dc21   CIP
                                                                          AC

Typography by Karin Paprocki

1 2 3 4 5 6 7 8 9 10

❖

First Edition

To my great-nephew Matthew
and a new century of hope

Lü, the fifty-sixth hexagram of
the *Book of Changes*.

"Be silent, be cunning, but above all be invisible."

PART ONE

CHAPTER | I

Joseph Young
Chinese Camp, Wyoming Territory
Sunday, June 14, 1885
Morning

F ather began the morning with his usual fight.

I tried to cling to a few more minutes of sleep because it was Sunday, our one day of rest. I could hear the stranger taunting Father outside the cabin. Most Chinese did when they found out Father's identity.

"So you're the high-and-mighty Otter," the man was jeering. "What are you doing stuck here digging coal just like me?"

Father's voice was as friendly as ever. "I thought my days with a pickax were done when I left the railroad," he agreed. "But here I am again."

I kept to my bed, hoping that this time it would be different: Father would be able to make peace with the man.

"And where are all your *American* pals now?" the man

sneered. "You told us they'd never let those laws pass."

"Those immigration laws passed only because of ignorance. My Western friends are fighting to overturn them right now," Father said to the man. "Westerners" was Father's polite word for *Americans*.

Calmly Father tried to assure the man that everything would work out for all of us eventually. He had such faith in *America* and in *American* justice. He never seemed to realize that his words, meant to soothe, only rubbed salt into old wounds. All the Chinese were frustrated with what was happening; but since they couldn't take it out on the *Americans*, they looked for other targets.

By now I was good at reading the tones and undercurrents of voices, so I knew that the man was getting ready to beat Father to a pulp.

With a sigh I unrolled my trousers, which I had been using as a pillow. Pulling them on, I rolled out of the bunk bed to save Father—sometimes it was hard to say who was raising whom.

The sun was just rising, so I made my way quietly past the other bunks, where our cabinmates were still snoring. When I stepped outside, I didn't recognize the man. The coal company kept upping our quotas and bringing in more Chinese to work. There were always plenty of Chinese who kept coming to the Land of the Golden Mountain—as they called *America*. And these guests—as they called themselves—were willing to do anything.

This guest was still plump with city fat. The coal mines would either slim him down or kill him. "I'm sick of your promises," he said, balling his hand into a fist.

Father just kept his hands at his sides, refusing to lift a hand to defend himself. As he said once, it was better for a Chinese to strike him than an *American*. He would get a beating if I didn't do something.

There was a small bench outside the cabin. Snatching it up, I brought it down hard on the newcomer's broad back; but he didn't fall down. He just stood there and gave a puzzled grunt.

And suddenly he became all the ungrateful fools who had driven us from San Francisco's Chinatown and who still made my life so miserable here. So I brought the bench down on his head this time.

The newcomer had a skull as hard as stone. He gave a shake of his head and whirled around, raising an arm to protect himself.

So I crouched, swinging the bench at his knee. With a shout, he went down, clutching his leg.

I bent over, hitting the newcomer again. He thrashed and wallowed like a beached whale. Then the bench, always a little wobbly, finally broke into halves. I got ready to flail at the newcomer with a piece in either hand.

Father, though, pinned my arms against my sides. "That's enough. If he can't work today, he won't get paid."

He'd gotten flabby as an interpreter in San Francisco,

but twelve- and even sixteen-hour shifts in the coal mines had restored his muscles. He said he was as strong now as when he worked on the railroads as a teenager. And he easily jerked me away.

Then he squatted over the newcomer. "Are you all right?"

I threw the pieces of bench away. As smart as Father was, he kept ignoring the truth. "Why do you care about him?"

Father gave me a reproachful look over his shoulder. "All Chinese are our brothers. Now please get some water." Then he helped the newcomer to sit up.

All the drinking water in the camps and in town had to be brought in by train. Though there was a creek, the water was so bad that you couldn't drink it. Going to the barrel, I took off the lid and picked up the dipper that hung from a nail.

On the surface of the water I saw my face floating against the sky. My jaw was square like Father's, but my eyes were small with sharp folds at the corners like Mother's. In San Francisco I had been careful to keep the hair shaved from the crown of my head; but here I'd let it grow out like many of the other miners. My skin was darker than theirs because I spent more time walking in the open.

Then my reflection disappeared as I lowered the dipper in and brought it over to the newcomer.

Sulking, the newcomer knocked it aside. "Get away from me," he mumbled. He looked a little wobbly as he rose, but he stumbled back to his cabin somehow.

Father tried to hide his hurt by making a joke. "Well, there's nothing like a brisk morning workout to get my appetite up. I hope White Deer will be cooking up something good."

Father could be so exasperating at times. He still held on to his past, a past in which everyone in Chinatown had wanted his help. Why couldn't he admit the truth? As far as all the Chinese were concerned, we were beneath the scum in the gutter. Maybe it would have killed him. But going on with this fantasy could get us killed too.

Though it was only dawn, the Wyoming air was already warm as a blanket, and the day's boilers hadn't even fired up yet. The shacks of our mining camp sat like mangy wooden buffalo huddling for the night, facing the glow on the horizon.

I was thirteen in Chinese years. Twelve in Western. And I was already as good as dead. I just had to get away from here. And then in the distance I saw the tip of the pinnacle that was Star Rock.

I'd go there.

CHAPTER | 2

Michael Purdy
Rock Springs, Wyoming Territory
Sunday, June 14, 1885
Morning

"Lord, I need air," Ma said, fanning herself with her hand. She yanked open the back door and gazed at the endless sky. "Not a lick of a breeze." There was only more dusty heat.

The sun was beginning to haul itself above the horizon, and the air was turning gold to red to purple. Like someone spilled a whole bunch of paint.

Pretty sunrises were wasted on Ma, though. She just heaved a sigh big enough to crack her spine. "Not a cloud in sight."

My spoon clinked against the bowl's sides as I tried to stir my porridge. Ma's porridge had more lumps than a toad has warts. "The almanac said there'd be no rain this month."

Ma turned from the doorway, using the bottom of her long apron to mop her forehead. "It's a mean day. It's the kind of day that makes dogs fight and men die."

I could feel it too, the hairs on the back of my neck tingling like the hairs of an angry cat. I'd have to be careful when I went outside. "Yes'm."

Ma shuffled over to me. On this warm morning her body gave off heat fiercer than a stove. "Land, is that all you're going to eat?"

I gave up trying to unlump my breakfast. Ma could burn water, let alone ruin porridge. I let go of the spoon, but it stood straight up in the stiff, sticky porridge. "Yes'm."

Poor Ma looked like she was already wore out and the day wasn't even begun yet. She lifted the porridge like it weighed a ton and set it in the pantry. "Well, I'm sorry, Mike; but what fussy children don't eat for breakfast they'll eat for supper."

My belly was growling like an angry dog, but I only said, "Yes'm." I didn't blame Ma, though, for being so snippy, because all our troubles were my fault.

When we heard the knock at the front door, Ma jerked her head at me. "See who that is, Mike."

I left the kitchen, heading through Ma's bedroom to the front room that served as both our parlor and my bedroom. The shack we lived in was called a shotgun, because you could stand at the rear door and blast a shotgun out the front door and not hit anything. There was no hallway, just doors opening from one tiny room to the next. But the shack did have a basement, where we washed the clothes.

When I opened the street door, I saw two of Ma's fellow laundrywomen, Mrs. Reilly and Mrs. Duval. Mrs. Reilly was a bareheaded blond woman with skin that never tanned, only turned a brighter shade of red. Though we were hardly into summer, she already looked like a lobster. "Morning, Mike." She measured me with her eyes. "My, you're getting as big as my Seth."

I wished I was big enough to stop his bullying. Too bad he couldn't be as kind as his ma.

"Yes'm," I said cautiously.

She knew how things were between me and her son. "I wish you two could get along," she said with a sad little shake of her head.

I was willing. The trouble was that Seth wasn't. We got along like two wildcats tied together by the tail and dumped inside a small bag. However, until the last few years, he'd contented himself with words.

Ma came into the parlor. "Don't fess yourself, Emma. Boys will be boys."

Mrs. Reilly turned guiltily toward Ma. "Honestly, Mary, I just don't know what to do with my boy. If I've told him once, I've told him a thousand times: Get along with Michael. But Seth's been so wild since his pa up and left."

It was about that time that he commenced to using fists rather than insults on me. Worse, he'd gathered up other boys whose pas had lit out or gotten laid off.

"If the Chinese hadn't stolen his job, he could've stayed,"

Mrs. Duval said. She was a small, dark woman with eyebrows that formed a solid line across her forehead. I could vaguely remember her laughing a lot when I was small; but the last few years all she did was frown—like her mouth was filled with old, dark, bitter coffee grounds.

"It's time we got rid of the pests, Justine," Mrs. Reilly agreed.

The heat made Ma rub her neck like she had a rash. "I think there's just enough tea for three."

"Well, thank you kindly." Mrs. Reilly held up a jar of green, cigarlike objects and announced, "The Shaw brothers paid me in cucumbers. Thought you might like a jar."

Ma clicked her tongue sympathetically. "Hardly anyone pays in hard coin."

Mrs. Duval started on her favorite pastime. "Things were fine before those Chinese came."

"Isn't that a fact," Ma agreed.

Their one hobby was complaining about the Chinese. To hear them flap on, Rock Springs was paradise before the Chinese came ten years ago.

I'd heard it all before. But Rock Springs was never Heaven on Earth—Chinese or no.

As Mrs. Reilly and Mrs. Duval hurried past, I felt sorry Ma was trapped here. I'd made a real hash out of her life. Things would have been real different for her if I hadn't been born. Pa might have hung around all the time before he died; and then she'd have had a real garden and her fireplace and her pet dog instead of just drawings.

When we'd first moved into this house, Ma had even sketched out the outline of a fireplace in pencil. "Your pa will build it there when he comes to stay for good," she had said.

And then she had outlined where she would hang her pictures when we had the money and drawn a rug on the floor.

"And can I have a dog?" I had asked.

So she had drawn that on top of the rug. And then on a fancy she had gone outside and drawn flowers and a picket fence on the front of our house.

But Pa had always left, and then one day he never came back. So all we had was the house and a lot of promises and the outlines of furniture and a garden and a happy life. Our feet had scuffed out the pencil dog and rug. Even the fireplace and pictures had smudged, so they looked more like dirt tracks. And the future . . . well, that was pretty smeared too.

We should have wiped them off a long time ago; but first we still hoped. Then we were too busy. Now we were too tired. So the furniture and the garden and the future still hung around, reminding me of what could have been if it hadn't been my fault—like ghosts you see but cannot touch. Sad ones you can't get shut of.

I tried to turn away, but that didn't do any good because I caught sight of myself in the glass of the window. Ma called my head pear shaped, with round cheeks and a narrow forehead. I had her freckles across my nose, but I had my pa's blue eyes and wispy blond hair. My reflection looked even more ghostly than the room. It was my fault that all this was happening.

I couldn't stand all that misery, so I finally stepped outside. As I closed the door behind me, I saw the tall church spire stabbing at the sky. I thought of the cool shadows and the quiet inside before services. I'd find some peace there.

The clean, whitewashed walls gleamed in the bright sunlight as I tried the doors. They were open and I stepped inside; but as I headed for a pew, a voice cracked like a whip.

"What are you doing here, Michael?" Miss Virginia asked. Miss Virginia was the minister's older daughter. She wasn't so much fat as big boned. I had never seen her in anything but starched whites. And she wore so many clothes, even in summer, that she rustled like an autumn tree when she walked. Her only decoration was at her throat—a pink-and-white cameo of her mother in silhouette. She always wore that.

She stood with a stack of books in her arms. I guess she'd been setting them out for the services later.

"I was just going to set a spell," I said.

"I have so many things to do to get the pews ready," she said as sweet as you please; but there was a point to her words as sharp as any knife's. "You'd just be in the way."

I reckon salvation don't matter on which portion of me

touched the church—feet or backside. "What if I just stand in the back then?"

"You're welcome to use the church any day but Sunday." She smiled. "You understand, Michael. Not all of our congregation are as open-minded as my family."

"Yes'm," I mumbled. "I'll leave way before anyone comes."

Miss Virginia sighed. "Thank you, Michael. Some people simply can't accept what you are."

Bastard. Bastard. Bastard. I could feel the word pounding with the beat of my heart. That's all I was to the folk of Rock Springs. I could feel my ears burning like red-hot coals.

There were times when the town felt as tight as last year's shirt, and I wanted to holler at the townsfolk that it wasn't my fault Pa hadn't married Ma. However, in this small town I might just as well have had the word "bastard" burned on my forehead like a cattle brand.

And top of the town's heap was Miss Virginia. She made sure everyone knew how charitable she was in letting a sinful woman and her bastard wash Miss Virginia's soiled clothes. Just as she made sure everyone knew how kind she was to teach English and the Lord's word to the Chinese miners.

I wanted to argue with her that if anyone should be here, it was a sinner like me. But we needed Miss Virginia's custom. Because of her, other folks were willing to let us do their clothes. So I reminded myself that Ma would have been a lot better off if she had dumped me on the nearest doorstep. Choking down some humble pie, I said, "Yes'm."

As I stepped outside again, my heart thumped inside my ribs like a bird trapped in a cage. Like it would bust.

I had to get out of Rock Springs. I had reckoned on hiring onto the railroad when I was eighteen. But I couldn't wait. I had to leave.

Now.

So I shanked it until I left the last building behind me and the sky could open up.

In the town, surrounded by houses and people, the sky felt all closed up like a clam. It was only on its outskirts, where nothing but scrubby brush grew, that I could feel how big the sky was. No buildings, no trees, just stunted brush.

I couldn't go to the north because of the cliffs. And to the south were the hills.

To the west then or east, where the wasteland stretched on and on, like it always had and always will.

And then I saw the pinnacle, taller than any church spire. I reckon no one cared if I set there till Doomsday.

CHAPTER | 3

Joseph Young
On the way to Star Rock
Sunday, June 14
Morning

After we went back inside the shack where everyone was just waking up, I waited impatiently for White Deer to cook our breakfast and then ate it as quickly as I could.

When I began to get my things together, Father looked up from his bowl of rice. "Where are you going?" he asked.

"I thought I'd add to my collection," I said carefully. I just needed to escape this place, and him, for a while.

He placed some pickled vegetables in his mouth with chopsticks. "Well, don't go far. We may go into the mines."

"But it's Sunday," I said, frustrated. "And the company doesn't need that much coal in the summer."

Father chewed slowly. "We can save the coal for the winter and sell it then, when the demand is high." There had been such a need for coal last winter that we'd worked twelve to sixteen hours a day, so I'd almost forgotten what the sun looked like.

I looked at him, worried. My nursemaiding job never stopped. He was pale and his face was worn, and the calluses on his fingers made him hold his chopsticks awkwardly. "Don't you think you've earned a day off?"

"Well, I could use the rest, but"—Father looked at me apologetically—"your cousins need money." My cousins were Great-uncle Foxfire's children.

I frowned. "They asked for money in their last letter, didn't they?" It was the same as always.

Father clicked the tips of his chopsticks tight. "Your grandfather Squeaky didn't want to, but Grandmother Cassia tightened the purse strings."

My grandmother Cassia was the head of our family back in Three Willows in China, where Father had been born. My grandfather Squeaky had been blinded in an accident when he and Father were building the railroad many years ago. Though Father hadn't visited them in many years, he still thought of them—but to me they were just names.

I cradled my sack in my arms. "We've sent home a fortune by now." I could feel the old resentment growing again.

"And your grandmother's invested wisely, but she's put your cousins on an allowance," Father said. He set his bowl down and sipped some tea.

"No wonder, the way they go through money," I said indignantly. "Grandmother should have done it a long time ago."

Even though they sucked us dry, Father defended them. "They have a certain standing that they have to keep up. They say the allowance isn't enough."

"It's a waste to send them any more," I said. Father could be as pigheaded about the family as he could be about the other guests. "Grandmother's always complaining that they gamble their money away."

Even before the troubles in Chinatown, it had been an old argument with Father.

Father hid his face in his rice bowl. "It's a debt I owe Uncle Foxfire," he mumbled.

"You must have paid it back by now," I said, exasperated. We had been making sacrifices all my life because of our spendthrift cousins. "When can we stop thinking of them and start thinking of ourselves?"

"I'm sorry," Father said. He ran a hand sheepishly down the back of his head. "I did something very foolish when I was young, and Uncle Foxfire saved my life at the cost of his. I have to take care of his family."

It was like Father to take the blame rather than place it where it belonged: on my cousins. Our family in China had been taking advantage of him for years; and now, when we needed their help the most, all they could do was make more demands. They'd work Father into an early grave yet. "What's the point of digging coal today? You said they need money now, but you can't sell it yet."

He hefted his left leg on top of his right knee and looked at his boot. "I bet I can get a few more months out of these." The soles were practically falling off his old boots, but I knew he would nurse them along—even if it meant tying string around them to hold them together. "The money I save on boots can help for now, and they can borrow the rest and pay it off in the winter when we do sell the coal. So come back soon, Precious Light."

It was an old game with us. I refused to respond to my Chinese name. Father wouldn't admit I had an American name. I'd chosen it myself, because I was an American, too, born and raised here.

But at the moment Father's stubbornness had used all my patience. "It's Joseph," I reminded him.

"Your Chinese name will always be Precious Light," he said.

"But I'm an *American*," I insisted. "I was born here. I grew up here. So all I need is an *American* name."

The matter would have rested there, but our cabin-mates had to butt in right then. Squirrel sat up in the bunk above and let his legs dangle over the sides. He'd gotten his nickname for his bushy queue. "American-born have no br-brains," he stuttered.

Spinner, White Deer's partner in the coal mines, rapped a knuckle against the side of his head. "Th-that's because their heads are hollow, like bamboo, right?" He was always quick with a joke. Maybe too quick.

Squirrel's partner, Bull, rose on his elbow from his bunk. His neck was as thick as a tree trunk. "You can ape those white demons all you want, but they'll never think you're one of them."

Ever since we had got here, the camp had picked on me as much as they had on Father. Suddenly I felt the anger swelling inside me even hotter. "And if I went back to China, the Chinese wouldn't treat me as an equal either. They'd nag me just like all the other guests do."

A devout Buddhist, White Deer tried to compromise, as he always did. "Why can't you be both American and Chinese?" he suggested in his soft voice.

"Because then you become neither," Bull insisted stubbornly. His mind was as hard as the mountains they dug.

Father studied my stormy face and took pity on me. "I'll see you in a little bit." As I left, however, he couldn't resist adding, "Precious Light."

Guests were outside doing chores or lounging. Several were heading south the couple of miles to the little Chinatown in Rock Springs.

I hurried past all of them before they could begin criticizing me. I was a half mile away before I realized I had forgotten to bring food and drink with me. I wasn't going to be able to stay out that long anyway.

Though it was only morning, my queue was already

feeling hot and sticky as it hung down my back like a lead chain. I hated the thing. The Manchus made all the Chinese wear it as a symbol of the horses that the Manchus had ridden when they had conquered us. It was death for a Chinese not to have a queue in China; but since I was never going to leave America, it was useless to me. However, Father insisted I keep it.

As I strode along, my shoulders felt lighter now that I'd escaped the old-timers telling me what to do and wear and say. One of these days I'd act like a real American and strike out on my own. No more bloodsucking family. No more rules. No more old-timers telling me how they did it in the old country. No more trying to make me into an antique. Just me. I'd do what I wanted when I wanted and I'd go where it pleased me, rolling along like a tumbleweed.

The sun had dried the ground hard as rock, and for a long time the only things to see were the low, pale-green bushes. And then I came across the string of dead rabbits.

"Dang," a boy shouted. "I missed."

"Give the sling to me, Fred," another boy said. "I'll get the varmint."

"There ain't time," the first boy protested.

I heard a stone whiz through the air.

"You couldn't hit a mountain with a boulder," the second boy complained. "Let someone use it who can shoot."

Six Western boys suddenly walked out of a fold in the land. One was a plump boy with a sling. "Well, hang it all. I made it."

A tall boy with hair as yellow as flame snatched the sling from the plump boy. "Well, it's mine now."

One of the other boys jabbed a finger at me. "A Chinaboy."

"This is better'n rabbits," the blond boy whooped.

I started to run.

CHAPTER | 4

Michael Purdy
Rock Springs
Sunday, June 14
Morning

Sometimes Bitter Creek was a lick and a promise, sometimes it flooded the town; but the water was always useless. Right now it was too deep to wade, so I crossed on the bridge and headed west.

For my landmark I picked out the pinnacle that towered over the hills. It reared upward from the soil like the Leviathan in the Bible, like some monster punished by being turned to stone. I'd learned every fold and fissure, just as I knew every worry line on my mother's face.

It was already so hot, it was hard to recognize things at a distance. The heat made their shapes all wavy. For a moment I thought they were the ghosts of the Shoshone Indians we white folks had driven away from here. I bet the Shoshone would have had something to say about the town's claim that this was "our" land. And I reckon the Shoshone would have wanted to drive us out back then just like we were trying to do to the Chinese right now.

I was a hundred yards from my landmark when I saw these greasewood bushes move. At least I had figured they were bushes. However, when they began to talk, I realized they were boys, their hollering thinned out over the distance into shrill yelps.

I should have turned around and hightailed it for home right then, but curiosity made me wait too long. By the time I realized it was Seth and his bully boys, it was too late.

"I think I see him," Fred shouted.

Right away I plopped down behind a sagebrush, heart pounding.

"Over here," Seth hollered.

I dropped to the ground, wishing I were a ghost myself. All I could do was scrabble across the hard dirt on hands and knees, not caring how much skin I scraped off on the gravel. I stayed in as much cover as I could, pausing only when I came to a clear space.

"There he is," Seth whooped.

The rabbit part of me wanted to stand up and run, but I made myself stay put. Seth's voice sounded fainter, as if he were moving away. They weren't after me. They were after someone else.

I almost laughed with relief when I had another scary thought. As far as Seth and his bully boys were concerned, I would make just as good a target.

I had to hide. If I could get to the pinnacle, I could hunker down among the boulders like a lizard. Getting down on my belly, I began to crawl. Like a snake. Like a worm. If I could have dug underground, I would have tunneled along like a gopher.

I paused every now and then and listened to the voices. My heart still thumped whenever they seemed to draw closer, and I lay still like some bird trying to hide itself from wolves. I must have grown ten years older before I reached the pinnacle.

At its base I started hunting around for a hiding place, when suddenly I saw the narrow hole in the wall. I'd never noticed it before. Ma was fond of saying that pride always goeth before the fall. I didn't know the pinnacle as well as I had figured.

I could still hear Seth and his bunch snuffling around, but from their voices, they were growing tired. The search had become too much like work, and they hated work as much as they hated soap. Even so, I couldn't be sure how long it would take them to skulk back to town.

Gratefully I felt the rim of the hole and hauled myself inside. The cave itself was low, so I crawled toward the shadows at the back.

Suddenly I heard something scrabble in the darkness. Was it a wolf? I didn't know which was worse: a wolf or Seth. Groping for a weapon, I found a rock and picked it up.

Then, in the dim light falling through the cave mouth,

I saw a Chinese about my age. He had his own rock in his hand and looked as dirty as I figure I did.

"This is my hiding place," I growled in a low voice

He spoke English clear as a bell. "I was here first."

I'd thought he'd talk broken, like the other Chinese. "You speak good," I whispered, blinking my eyes in surprise.

"I speak English well," he corrected me all high-and-mighty-like.

"Were they hunting you?" I asked.

"I know lots of hiding places," the boy said. "Have to. And since I spend so much time underground, I know a few things about caves."

I thought of how we were both Seth's punching bags and that gave us something in common. I took a chance and put my rock down. Then I held up my empty hands to show I was harmless. "Truce."

"Truce," he agreed, and let his rock thump on the ground too.

"So you're a miner?" I asked.

"It's just for a short while," he insisted.

We both looked relieved as the hunters' voices faded away in the distance. After a long silence I sighed. "I reckon they're gone. Seth and his bunch will head for town now and look for shade. We can leave."

The boy dug out a candle stub and a match. "Go where you like. I'm staying."

That puzzled me some. "I would have figured a miner

would want as much sunshine as he could."

"You can find sunshine anywhere, but not what I'm hunting." He lit the candle and set it on a rock in the back of the cave. On the cave floor was a sack. From it the boy took out a hammer and chisel.

"What critters are you going to catch with those?" I pointed at the tools.

"Stars." He began to crawl over toward a wall.

Was he joshing me? "In here?"

"Just watch." He paused by one spot, squinting at the wall.

I shifted so I could see what he was doing. "You're an odd duck, aren't you?"

The Chinese boy smiled sadly at me over his shoulder. "It's not just Americans hunting me."

"Chinese too?" I asked. When he nodded, I just had to shake my head. "But why?"

He studied the wall in front of him like he was studying a page in a book. "Why are you hiding from those other Americans?"

I didn't know anything about Chinese families, but I reckoned they'd think a bastard was a low-down skunk too. "They're no friends of mine."

"And these Chinese are no friends of mine either." He began to tap lightly at the wall. "It's dangerous to be different." Pebbles rattled down from his chisel.

"Amen to that." I crawled over to see better.

"There," he said with satisfaction. With the chisel he

gently pried a slab of stone from the wall and held it out toward me. "Take a look."

I leaned forward to look at his treasure. It looked like a clamshell, sure enough; but it gleamed bright and yellow. "Is that gold?" I asked, growing excited.

"Fool's gold," he said expertly. "Iron pyrite. Over the years the mineral takes the place of the real shell. See?"

As he swept the candle back and forth, the ceiling and walls glittered off more golden shells. "I call this place Star Rock even if it's mostly shells."

"They may be shells, but they shine like stars," I agreed. "A whole ocean of stars."

And I remembered one evening long ago when Ma and me had been hanging a big load of wash with the help of a kerosene lantern. Suddenly lights had flashed across the sky, and I had tried to get her to make a wish on one of the shooting stars. Ma had said she had tried wishing on a whole bushel of stars and nothing ever came of it.

The Chinese boy studied the shells all around us. "I don't know what they're doing here in the middle of the country, though."

I recollected something from my father's notebooks. "This whole area used to be an ocean long ago."

He got as excited as me. "I read about the big Flood in the Bible. Do you think it left these?" I guess Miss Virginia taught him Bible stories as well as English.

"Well, I don't know about that," I said, scratching my

head. "But over in another part of the state there are some professor types who are digging up these bones from these big critters. My pa said they call them dinosaurs. That means terrible lizard." I couldn't see why the professors couldn't have just called the critters that; but Pa just laughed. He said the more names a critter had, the fancier the pedigree; and that's what counted with easterners.

"Really?" he said, his eyes growing even bigger.

No one else in town cared about old lizards, no matter how big.

"My father used to dig for them too. I wonder if there are any lizards in here," I said, looking around us.

"All I've seen are shells and fish skeletons," he said. He swung his candle around, stopping at various places so I could see the skeletons of fish, tiny ones and big ones and weird-looking shellfish. There were plants, too, with strange shapes.

I just had to get one for Ma. Maybe if she had one in her hand, she'd start wishing again. Digging out my pocketknife, I started to lean toward a shell at the same time as the boy.

Our heads thunked together hard.

"Ow. You have a head like a rock," he complained, rubbing the sore spot.

"Yours must be solid bone," I said. I began to pick at the rock with my knife.

"That shell is mine," he snapped.

I went on stubbornly scraping at the rock, because this was for Ma. "I saw it first."

"But I found Star Rock first." Angrily he seized my wrist. "Get back." He raised his hammer in warning.

I pulled free, holding my knife up. "Find your own."

The anger flashed inside me like a match to a fuse. Mean, ugly thoughts whirled through my head: This boy was a greedy pig. He was trying to hog all the stars for himself.

And the anger just kept getting stronger and stronger until it was a howling windstorm inside me. And then it was like the trapdoor to a cellar banged open; and all these mean, hateful things hopped into my thoughts. I realized they were the things that Ma and Mrs. Reilly had said about the Chinese. I hadn't realized I had stored it all away inside, but I had; and like some white lightning, it had turned to pure poison.

The rage just poured out of me. "You Chinese just come storming into a place and taking whatever you like. You take the best coal rooms and steal coal. The worst of it is you take jobs that could go to Americans. There's a lot of families going hungry in town because of you."

He stiffened. "Our families are more than hungry. They're starving. Why do you think we put up with such miserable jobs? We work so they won't die."

We were both so mad now that we were panting like bellows.

I hated him. I hated the Chinese. I hated Seth. I hated the town.

But since he was the only one there, I wanted to pound him.

His face was so ugly, and the way it was all twisted now made it the ugliest I'd ever seen.

I raised my fist to punch him.

He lifted his hammer even higher—like he had the same notion. What right did he have to be mad? He was the thief. He was the invader.

I wondered if my face was just as ugly and twisted as his. And the anger melted away like dirt under Ma's strong soap.

I had been ready to kill him. And that scared me.

No way did I want to be like Seth, but it had been too close. I lowered my fist. "Take it, then, and much good may it do you."

I retreated to another part of the cave and began poking around and promising myself that next time I came here, I'd have my own hammer and chisel and candle.

Suddenly the steady tapping of the boy's hammer stopped. From the corner of my eyes I could see him huddling as he uncovered another treasure. I had to fight the urge to kick his backside and chase him from the cave.

That's what Seth would do, I told myself. You can do better. After all, there're fossils piled all around you. Find another.

I had to admire the way the boy worked. He was so careful and methodical. When he finally freed the slab from the rock, he cradled it in his hands. "Beautiful."

Even though I had wanted to ignore him, I could not resist peeking. It was a disk with golden rays shooting out from the middle to the sides. It looked just like the kind of star you'd wish on.

He held it up for me to admire. "Pretty, isn't it?"

I couldn't take my eyes off it. "I've never seen anything like it. What is it?"

"It's a type of shell too," he said.

"It looks like a star to me," I murmured. "I wish Ma could see this." Maybe it would make her smile again. Suddenly I wanted that more than anything.

"I don't remember my mother," he said, taking back the star. "She died when I was young."

"My father died too," I said.

Suddenly he thrust it toward me. "Here."

I knew if I touched it, I could not give it back. "No. But thanks for letting me look at it."

"No, you take it. For keeps. Start your own collection," he said, and set it down in front of him. "I've been digging here awhile." The boy traced the rays with a fingertip. "But this is one of the nicest I've ever seen."

I picked up the shell careful like. Afraid I'd break it, I brushed my fingers lightly over the golden surface. It was so beautiful that suddenly I felt overwhelmed by his kindness. "I don't have anything to give you back."

He tilted back his head and studied the shells overhead for a long while. When he finally spoke, his words were slow and thoughtful. "These don't belong just to me."

I cradled the star in my hands. "They don't belong to me either." It'd been stupid to get mad at him. I felt ashamed.

He turned with a grin. "Then we have to share."

I ran a finger over the shell. "That's the trouble outside the cave. No one shares."

He bit his lip as he hunted for the right words. "In here, Star Rock is separate from all that." He waved his hammer toward the cave mouth. I knew that he meant the town and the mining camps and all the fighting between his kind and mine.

I nodded slowly. I felt like I was inside our own little bubble beneath an ocean as old as Creation. Inside here, I felt . . . well, peaceful. "My ma told me this story once. There are these little fellows called elves, and they live in this magic cave. Time works different in there than outside."

He stared at the entrance. It looked like the door into a hot stove, it was so different from the cool, quiet shadows in here. "When I'm in Star Rock, the outside doesn't matter."

I thought about that a moment. In here there was no Seth, no Miss Virginia. It didn't matter what I was. It didn't matter that he was Chinese. "It's nice to get away from everything."

"It feels . . . well, almost normal," he agreed.

I shut my eyes. "No, more than that. Star Rock's different. My friend, Miss Evie, lets me read some of her books. And it's like living in a new place with a new me. The kids in the stories are always so happy and their friends and family are so nice."

"And in the end everything comes out happy," he said sadly—as if for him, too, there couldn't be a happy ending.

As much as I didn't want to admit it, despite the funny eyes and skin, he was a little like me. "You're not bad for a Chinese," I grunted.

"And you're not a monster after all," he said grudgingly.

It annoyed me that he'd ever entertained the notion; but I kept hold of my temper. "Since we're both likely to bump into one another here, I guess we got to work something out."

He chewed on the idea some; and his mouth twisted down like he found it awfully sour; but he was pretty sensible for a Chinese. He studied me for a moment and then suddenly thrust out his hand. "My name's Joseph Young."

"Michael Purdy," I said, and we shook hands solemnly.

We sat in an awkward silence for a spell. Finally, he cleared his throat. "I have to get back."

"Me too," I said, and then said to him, "I reckon I'll be here next Sunday." I think it was half warning and half invite.

I felt like the biggest fool when he ignored me and crawled toward the mouth of the cave, dragging his sack with him. As he reached the lip, he twisted around and nodded. "See you."

And he disappeared through the opening to the outside.

CHAPTER | 5

Joseph Young
Chinese Camp
Sunday, June 14
Late afternoon

All the way back to camp, I kept wondering about Michael. Why weren't the other Western boys friends with him? After all, he looked and talked just like them. I suppose it was just as well for me that he was different: If he had been like them, he would have pounded me.

The cabin was empty when I got back. Father must have gone to dig coal, and the others must have gone with him.

It's funny. Michael had made me forget my anger, but now that the fury was gone, it left room for the guilt to rush in. I should have come back sooner. I really should have been helping Father like I always had back in Chinatown. In those days we'd been a team, for even when I was young I'd helped Father as his secretary.

Ever since Father had come to the Land of the Golden Mountain, he'd studied Western customs and laws as well as its language and made many friends among the Westerners. Up until a few years ago everyone in San Francisco's Chinatown turned to him to interpret not only the language but also the laws and customs of the Land of the Golden Mountain.

Which was hard, because so many Westerners hated us. They kept passing laws meant to drive us away. But the worst was a few years ago, when they tried to stop any Chinese from coming to America or allowing any Chinese already here to become citizens.

Father had argued that such a law was illegal by America's own Constitution. You couldn't single out just one specific group for such harshness.

And our American friends sided with us, especially Uncle Sean. Father had met him when they were both boys working on the railroad. I liked Uncle Sean, who had studied Chinese as earnestly as Father had studied Westerners.

With Sean's encouragement, Father had gone everywhere, organizing Chinese and raising money to stop the passage of the law. He staged rallies all over the state.

When the law had passed anyway, Father had lost all face with the other guests. Worse, since they couldn't take out their anger on the Americans, they took it out on us. We had dropped from the top of Chinatown to the gutter, and we had wound up here in the coal mine. But even here we couldn't escape Father's notoriety. Once the miners learned who he was, Father was lower than the mud on their boots. Everyone, like the newcomer this morning, mocked us for what had happened instead of blaming the Westerners.

I should have gone to the coal mine, but I thought resentfully of my fat cousins back in China. Maybe it was time I took my own advice to Father. I'd think of myself for a change rather than the leeches in China.

So even though I felt wicked, I stayed right where I was. After I had some leftovers, I opened up the gunnysack and took out my treasures. I had never seen one lovelier than Michael's shell, and for a moment I was sorry that it wasn't in my collection after all.

Whenever I went through the shells, I thought of Mother. She had loved the ocean. If she'd been alive, she would have liked Star Rock just as much, I think.

When I got out my box with my collection, it seemed to weigh almost as much as a sea now; and I added my finds from today. Then I stowed it away.

I wondered what Michael was doing with his finds. At least he had a mother to give them to.

I'd never told Father about Star Rock. I wasn't sure if he wanted me to wander that far, so I'd never wanted to risk it. He'd just assumed I found the fossils nearby. Star Rock had been my special place—mine alone, until Michael.

I realized then that I couldn't tell Father about the Western boy. He would have started asking about the cave and all the risks; and that would have drawn it into the ugly outer world where everyone was fighting with the Westerners.

Star Rock had to be protected from the outside. I had to have some peace somewhere.

With a sigh I put everything away and got my gear. It was time to help Father.

CHAPTER | 6

Michael Purdy
Rock Springs
Sunday, June 14
Late afternoon

I t was on the tip of my tongue to tell Ma about Joseph
and Star Rock as soon as I got home, but she popped
up out of the cellar, her sleeves rolled up and her arms
red as lobsters. "Thank Heaven you finally came back. Mr.
Kincaid dropped off a huge load of laundry and needs it
back by tomorrow." Then her eyes dropped to the floor.
"Oh, Mike."

I looked behind me and saw the dirty footprints across
the boards. I'd been so excited that I'd plumb forgotten to
come in the back way and take off my shoes. "I'm sorry, Ma."

"You always are." Ma wearily wiped a sudsy hand across
her forehead. "Where were you? I really needed your help."

"But it's Sunday," I protested.

"I know, Mike. I'd love a rest as much as you, but . . ."
Ma waved her hand and suds flew off her fingertips. "We

can't lose Kincaid to the Chinese too." She looked so tired and yet so scared right then that suddenly I felt like a traitor for spending time with Joseph.

A long train rumbled by at that moment, like thunder on wheels. While everything in the house rattled, I felt the shell weighing down my pocket.

I should have told her about it; but if I did, she'd find out about the boy I'd met, and she hated the Chinese so. She'd never let me go to Star Rock again. And even if I felt like the lowest traitor to Ma, I couldn't let that happen.

When the train was gone, I fibbed, "I'm sorry, Ma. I went out for a walk and fell asleep."

"And what if wolves had got ahold of you?"

"Maybe you'd be better off if the wolves had got me," I said.

Ma stared at me, surprised. "What's gotten into you?"

"Well, wouldn't you?" I asked. I wanted to hear something sweet, like most mothers would say.

Ma looked hurt, and her mouth quivered. I could feel myself inside saying, Tell me you need me.

"You'd like a pillow sort of ma, wouldn't you?" Ma asked quietly. "I mean, somebody who was all soft and huggable."

"I wouldn't mind," I allowed.

"Well, a softer woman would have given up a long time ago."

"Yes'm," I said. Her words weren't fool's gold but the twenty-four-karat truth, and I knew it.

"I do it for you," Ma said. She clasped her hands in front of her as she lifted her shoulders. "If I'm not as nice as the other mothers, it's because I can't afford to be."

"Yes'm," I sighed.

Ma gave me a little shove. That's as close as she ever came to a loving touch. "What's done is done. Now get to work."

I wound up staying awake late to catch up with everything. And supper was that morning's porridge. The lumps seemed to have grown harder and bigger, but I choked it down because I didn't want to have to meet up with it tomorrow.

I didn't complain, though. While I ate, she was busy cleaning my tracks off the boards. It just about broke my heart to see her on her knees, because I knew how tired she must be. "I'll do that, Ma."

"No, no, you have your supper," she said. Her brush made swooshing sounds. "I let this go long enough. I won't have Emma thinking we live like pigs."

Poor Ma. All I seemed to bring her was a heap of trouble.

I had just washed the dishes when she was finishing her final chore: The last thing every evening, she wound Pa's big gold watch, which hung from a nail above the outline of the fireplace. I wasn't allowed to touch it.

I padded past her in my socks. "Night, Ma."

"Night, Mike," she sighed, and shuffled into her own room and shut her door.

As I lay down on my cot, Pa's big gold watch chimed.

The only other real thing on the wall was the framed photograph, which Ma had hung up on a nail so it stood above where the mantel would be someday.

I leaned forward to peer at the brown, faded photograph. The young girl smiled back at me. I had Ma's word that the happy girl was her when she was sixteen, because the girl didn't look anything like her now.

All I had of Pa's was his notebooks. He'd been a real college man, but he liked to hunt. Down by Como Bluff eight years ago a friend of his, Bill Reed, had found some huge bones. Bill Reed was a fellow hunter who had been hired to kill game for the railroad crews and had stayed on as a section foreman. He and the station agent had sold some bones to this big museum back east. I reckon those easterners got excited over the oddest things, because you couldn't use those bones even for soup; but they'd hired Bill Reed to dig out more.

I was glad when Pa said that the big lizards had all died away millions of years ago—probably of fright from looking at one another. Some were bigger than our house, with claws as long as my leg and teeth as long as my arm.

Hunting dinosaurs got to be as big a passion for Pa as hunting live animals. I think he was a little sad that he had missed out on shooting the dinosaurs. So he used to go down and help out his friend Bill, who did it for money; but Pa dug strictly as a hobby.

Then Pa would come back with notebooks full of drawings

of all sorts of bones and skulls. I could just see the dinosaurs tromping down Main Street and giving Seth and his bully boys a taste of their own medicine.

Because dinosaurs excited Pa, I took an interest in them too and wanted to know more about them. I picked up what I could in the schoolroom so I could figure it out myself. I stuck at it even though going to school left me open to a wheelbarrowful of insults and kicks outside the schoolhouse, because I was a bastard.

I dug one of his notebooks from under my bed and started to turn the pages. Finding an empty page, I wrote down where I had made my first find. Then I sketched the wishing star.

Just like Pa.

CHAPTER | 7

Joseph Young
Mine Number Six
Sunday, June 14
Late afternoon

Father didn't bother to scold me when I joined him in the mine.

From the Heaven of Star Rock I jumped straight into Hell. My teacher, Miss Virginia, says Hell will be full of fire. But I know better. Hell will be a coal mine.

Hell will be black dust that clogs everything—eyes, ears, and nose.

Hell will be trying to breathe the foul air. Your lungs will heave and heave but you'll still feel like you're suffocating.

It's hot in the coal mine, as if there are fires hidden just behind the wall.

It's blacker than night. It's blacker than coal. And all you have is a little light from the lamp on your head. And the lamp stinks almost as bad as you do.

Hell will be lying on your side swinging a pickax sideways while dust and bits of coal pile up all over you and turn you black.

My own personal patch of Hell was a "room" in the mine that I worked with Father. It was about twenty-four feet wide but only six feet tall.

You punch holes into the wall and blast, and then you shovel the black lumps into a cart while you try to breathe the swirling blast.

But Hell is also never knowing if the next moment is your last. Walls and ceilings can collapse, or you can get hit by a rock that happens to fall. I've heard stories about miners drowning when water floods in. And there's always the danger of gases.

Maybe the point of your pick will free gas that's been trapped for thousands of years. You can't smell it. You can't see it. You might see the dust suddenly eddying in a gust of it. And then it explodes when a stray spark sets it off. Four years ago thirty-five Chinese died in an explosion.

And that doesn't include the explosions when a powder charge gets set wrong.

All the miners worked in teams of two. We had almost starved the first month, until we'd gotten enough muscles and calluses. If it hadn't been for the kindness of our cabinmate, White Deer, we would have starved. We were all supposed to ante up for our food; but for a time he had paid our shares out of his own pocket.

We got paid by the ton. At our best, Father and I'd managed to mine nine tons in one day, but we only got money for six because that's all the company said was usable until demand went up in the winter.

From the corner of my eye I saw something moving in the dim light, and I barely dodged the ugly yellow teeth in time. The mule that pulled the pit car glared at me, waiting for its next chance.

Mules are the only things more exasperating than Father, and unlike him, they bite any chance they get.

At first I had gotten nipped every day.

I hate mules. I will always hate mules. I will hate them in my next life. I will hate them a thousand lives from now. And if I finally make it to Heaven and find even one mule there, I will back right out of the Gates and tell St. Peter, "No thank you."

But there isn't a chance any mule will ever make it to Heaven.

They'll all be in Hell, driving the Devil crazy.

CHAPTER | 8

Michael Purdy
Rock Springs
Monday, June 15
Early morning

G ood morn-ing," a voice said in heavily accented
English.

The hot sun almost blasted the eyeballs out
of my head, so I had to squint. It was Ah Lee. Though he
had a queue like all the Chinese did, he hid it under his hat.
I didn't know why. It wasn't like he could fool folks into
thinking he was an American.

Ah Lee must have been heading for his laundry, which
was the biggest in town.

"You up early. You work hard like me. Have candy." He
pulled a paper bag from his coat pocket.

If Ma had been around, I would have refused, because
he had stolen a lot of customers from us. Ten years ago,
when the railroad had brought the Chinese into Wyoming
to work in the mines, some of their kinfolk had tagged

along and set up laundries as well.

I had always judged candy was candy, but when I had taken it before, I had glared at him just to let him know that he couldn't buy my friendship with a penny sweet. He always pretended not to notice.

But today I was thinking over what Joseph had told me. Maybe Ah Lee was trying to support his family too. It was just too bad it had to be at our expense.

"Thank you," I said, taking one and putting it in my mouth.

He popped another into his own mouth as well. "Hmm, you like?"

I used my tongue to shove the candy against one cheek. "Yeah." Now that I had met Joseph, I was more curious about his kind. "Say, why do you put your queue under your hat?"

"So bad boys can't pull it," he said, yanking at an invisible queue. "But you not bad boy?"

I gave him a grunt because I knew the town's verdict on that; and I headed off quick so no one would see us together.

As sugary as the candy was, it lost its taste when I passed by Mr. Spenser, who was strutting out of town on his way to the mines. He was the supervisor of all of them and used to give us his custom. But he had switched to Ah Lee. All those mining people stuck up for the Chinese. The railroad people did too, because the railroad not only used Chinese work crews but owned the mines where the other Chinese worked.

Still, I smiled and nodded politely like Ma had told me to do; he just looked through me.

Even when I used to bring him his laundry, he had tried his best to ignore me. Like I was a ghost.

I kept the smile on my face though. I'd had lots of practice at it. Most of the respectable folk treated me like I was the ghost boy. They didn't want to see me—let alone talk to me—and probably wished I'd haunt some other town.

I've read that other towns and cities have real streets that get laid out straight and true, with all the buildings lined up in rows; but our town just sort of happened. When they opened up the mines, the railroad built tracks right away so they could get the coal; and the miners plunked down their tents wherever they liked. We didn't start out as more than a coal camp that grew up around the railroad tracks; but as wood and stone took the place of canvas, Rock Springs swelled up into a proper town.

The streets wandered back and forth over the old mine tunnels. It was a wonder they didn't cave in. And I'd never heard of any other town that had so many railroad tracks running down its main road, which folks were beginning to call Front Street. It was a broad avenue with several tracks running parallel to one another. There were always engines and cars moving up and down and in and out, so you had to hop lively to cross it.

The water train had come in from Green River, and the deliverymen were filling the barrels of the wagon to deliver to folks. I walked around it and paused to watch one long train creak and rumble slowly along, wondering where it was heading. Somewhere far, I bet.

Johnson and diGiorgio were already perched outside Kincaid's Mercantile in their usual spots. When they'd had their jobs at the mines, they'd been regular customers of ours. Now their families either washed their own, or—from the look of their clothes—just went dirty.

I grinned at them and dipped my head, but they simply watched me pass with sullen eyes. Keep smiling, ghost boy, I told myself. Keep smiling.

One day I'd get shut of this town. I'd go someplace far away. Today even California seemed too close to Rock Springs. What if Seth followed me there?

I needed to light out for some really distant country. Like China. I'd ask Joseph about that this Sunday.

CHAPTER | 9

Joseph Young
Mine Number Six
Monday, June 15
Late morning

Father punched a hole into the wall, or "face," of our room in the pit, using his hands to twist the bit while his chest pressed against the flat plate at the auger's end.

While I waited by the entrance, I picked up a piece of coal. In the lamplight the coal looked like a lump of the night sky, solid black and shiny all over. I turned it in my palms, seeing the little rainbow colors glisten on its sides.

Other Chinese had rooms next to us; and when they could, they liked to play the Game.

"Here's another piece of bottomland back home. Right?" Spinner called down the tunnel from his room. I heard the thump of coal into a cart. He must be shoveling it in now.

I heard more thuds as someone else loaded coal. "And

here's duck for dinner for my family," White Deer agreed in a voice so low it was hard to hear him.

Squirrel was piling coal from his room into a different cart. "And a w-w-window on the house," he announced.

I'd never been to China, but from the talk in Chinatown and in the camp, I knew more than I wanted to about it.

It was only morning, but Father already looked tired. Even so, he forced himself to smile as he pulled out the auger. "And a new flower garden for Grandmother Cassia."

The lamp on my cap was starting to flicker, so I dropped the coal and took the lamp pick from my pocket, tugging at the cotton wick until it burned steadily again.

The others were running through a new set of imaginary purchases when White Deer nodded to me. He was the only one who was really friendly to us; but he had to be because of his Buddhist beliefs, which said you had to be nice to everything, even bugs. "This piece's for you." He asked me gently, "What do you want to buy for your family in China?"

I set my cap back on my head and then stared at my grimy hands, wondering if I would ever get all the black dust out of them. And I thought how my cousins sat around with lily-white fingers because I did all the work. "They get enough from us. Why should I buy them any more?"

Bull banged his shovel against the cart. "Do you think this is some kind of joke, boy? You owe everything to your family. We have to do this for them. My family was starving before I came here to work."

"M-m-mine too," Squirrel said. He was as small as Bull was big, and he was never far from Bull. "Between the taxes and rents, my family barely had enough to eat even in a good year. And one year out of a three was bad: plagues, wars, droughts, floods."

In the corridor there was pile of rock—bits of slate, dirt, and slack coal that was useless for burning—that Americans called gob. I sat down on it now. "Well, nowadays my family seems more worried about redecorating than eating," I said.

White Deer placed a metal plate with his number on his cart so he would get credit for it. It was an effort for him to raise his voice so we could all hear him. "But their home is your home too." He gave me an encouraging smile. "You must want something there."

"I never want to see China," I said.

It was always a mistake to speak the truth to guests. They all looked shocked.

"B-b-but you're Chinese!" Squirrel protested. "You c-c-can't stay here for forever. The w-white demons won't let you. They've been driving us out of Chinatowns all around this awful country." White demons was what the others called Americans.

Bull plucked some slack from the cart and threw it to the side. "And killing the ones they can catch," he said with a scowl.

Father came out of the room rubbing his chest. "You'll like China once you see it."

"Never," I insisted.

"You let him get away with too much, Otter. If my boys tried to talk crazy like that, I'd slap them into the next county," Bull growled.

I turned to eye Bull. "I'm sure your sons would love to have you come home to China. What do you know about raising children? You've been here most of their lives."

Bull started as if the truth stung, but Father put a hand on my shoulder. "That's enough of that." He pulled me down the tunnel until he could speak in a lower voice. "What you just did to Bull isn't kind."

"But it's the truth," I said sullenly.

"I know," Father agreed, and glanced at the huge, glowering man. "But guests need their dreams. That's what gets them through these hard days."

"What about my dreams?" Angrily I waved my hands around the tunnel. "Do you think I want to be here?"

"We'll just have to manage somehow." Father sighed.

But it was getting harder and harder.

CHAPTER | 10

Michael Purdy
Rock Springs, Wyoming
Monday, June 15
Late morning

When the door of the church rectory opened, Miss Evie stepped out.

In her crisp white dress, with her golden hair hanging loose, she looked like an angel. She was the minister's younger daughter and my classmate in school. "Morning," she said. She smelled of scented Florida water.

"Hello," I answered in surprise. My own voice suddenly got as shrill as a bird's. "Thank you for the colored papers." She'd given me a pile of different-colored papers last week.

"I wasn't using them, and I thought your mother could use them for leaflets. You know, let everyone know about your business." She held her basket in front of her with both hands. "The summer's going by too fast. Soon we'll be back in mean old Miss Pritchett's hands."

It couldn't go by fast enough for me. I liked school—

which was the only time I could escape from the hill of dirty laundry at home. And even if Miss Pritchett treated me like a pile of dung that had suddenly been dumped into the schoolroom, she had enough conscience to teach me.

Books didn't judge you. They let anyone have their knowledge. You just had to open them up. They took me to faraway lands without caring what I was. So I went on putting up with Miss Pritchett's snippy little comments and the bullyragging of the other children.

Suddenly Miss Virginia showed up behind Miss Evie. "Oh, Michael, I'm glad to see you. I'm afraid the last batch of clothes your mother did was ... well, just not quite up to snuff." Her voice grew ever so sweet. "Do you think she'd mind doing them again?" It was more a command than a question, though. "You can pick them when you drop off our other bundle."

"Yes'm," I said.

"We should be back from the store in a bit," Miss Evie said brightly. "Just knock on the front door."

Miss Virginia smiled tolerantly. "Or would you prefer the back door, Michael?"

Miss Evie was one of the few who treated me like a real person. "Why can't he use the front door like everyone else?"

Miss Virginia gave a friendly shrug. "We've talked about that already. Haven't we, Michael?"

"The Bible says—" Miss Evie began indignantly.

Miss Virginia cut her off with a laugh. "Don't go quoting

the Good Book to me, missy. Who almost flunked out of Sunday school?"

Miss Evie flushed. "You didn't grade fair."

Miss Virginia appealed to me for sympathy. "Anyway, Michael, you don't want to make things awkward for us, do you?"

Because Miss Evie was there, I almost told Miss Virginia what I really thought. But I couldn't do that for Ma's sake because, despite all her highfalutin ways, we couldn't afford to lose Miss Virginia.

"Yes'm," I mumbled.

Miss Evie looked puzzled. With her fine clothes and comfortable house, she could not understand why I was backing down. "Aren't you going to stand up for yourself?" she asked me.

Easy for her to wonder, impossible for a bastard to do.

I couldn't look at her. "No'm," I said helplessly.

"Michael Purdy, I thought you had sand in your craw," Evie sniffed. Her scorn hurt far worse than any kick, any insult.

I wasn't a fool though. "No'm." It was less difficult the second time. And it would be even easier the third time and on and on until it became second nature. I had to get out of this town before that happened.

Miss Virginia nodded her head with satisfaction at a job well done. She liked learning folks, especially if they were little sisters and bastards. "Come, Evie. We want to get to the mercantile before they sell out of that new damask. I have to be back in time to teach my boys."

Confused and hurt, Miss Evie glanced at me as she followed her sister. I stuck around the rectory until the last of Evie's scent faded away from the dusty air.

I wished it was Sunday already. At Star Rock I could forget it all.

CHAPTER | 11

Joseph Young
Mine Number Six
Monday, June 15
Early afternoon

We were outside our room in the pit, waiting for the dust to settle from the explosion. Father took his scissors and a piece of paper from the back pocket of his denims. Then, bending his head so his lamp could shine on his hands, he began to snip out one of his cutouts.

In the good old days back in Chinatown, his desk had been littered with paper dragons and flowers and butterflies; and there were always little bits of paper clinging to his clothes and even his hair. I used to have to groom him before I could let him walk through Chinatown.

Of course, back then he had used choice sheets of paper. Nowadays he settled for anything, including old newspapers. A half-finished cutout of a fish lay on the ground.

59

"Why don't you relax," I suggested. If anything, Father looked worse than before.

"Because I like doing this. It reminds me of China," he said, picking up the fish. "You should have seen my uncle Foxfire. His cutouts used to come to life."

"You ought to rest your eyes, at least," I coaxed.

"Well, I won't be doing this for much longer. My fingers aren't as supple anymore." He stared at the calluses. "In a few months I'll be lucky if I can manage to cut out circles. And anyway, this is for Spinner's son. He wants him to be a scholar."

In China, the story goes that if a carp can swim up a certain river and pass through a certain gate, it can become a dragon. Scholars used it as a symbol because it reminded them to study hard. But Father had used the carp for his disastrous protest campaign against the new immigration laws.

I sighed. "I'm sick of them by now. You must have printed up a thousand posters with a picture of a carp; and I think I covered every wall in Chinatown with them."

Father's hand cradled the carp as if it were alive. "You don't reach the gate without some setbacks."

I shook my head. "Why are you doing Spinner any favors? He makes fun of us all the time. He only asked you to do this because he's too cheap to buy his son a real present."

Father went on cutting. "He'll change. So will all of

them. You just have to be patient a little longer. "

Frustrated, I folded my arms. "You keep telling me that there's a rainbow behind the next cloud; but every time we look, there's only more clouds.

"If you give up looking, you'll never find it." He smiled maddeningly.

Right then Mr. Spenser, the mine superintendent, came along and started to assign new rooms in the mine. We got Number One, and Bull and Squirrel got Room Two.

"I've been chewing on this idea for a while. It makes sense to put my best workers where they'll get the most coal," Mr. Spenser said in English.

Mr. Eagleton was one of the two pit bosses for our section of the mine. *"Where do you want them to go?"*

Mr. Spenser fingered his chin. It was so pale compared to ours, blackened by the coal. *"What about Steve's? That room is wasted on that lazy idiot. They can switch."*

"Steve isn't going to like it," Mr. Eagleton warned.

Mr. Spenser shrugged. *"I'm fed up with Steve. He's been trouble for us from the first day we hired him. If he complains, get rid of him."*

We had been shoveling coal into a cart and had stopped to listen. *"But that isn't right,"* Father objected.

"Are you trying to tell me what to do, John?" Mr. Spenser demanded. Mr. Spenser called all Chinese John.

"I'm just trying to work out something that's fair to everyone," Father explained patiently. *"The Western crews are just trying to*

support their families like us."

Mr. Spenser jabbed a finger at his chest. *"I say who digs where and when. It's my neck if the mine doesn't make money. You sabe me, John?"*

"What did you say?" Bull asked Father in Chinese.

Father didn't look too happy when he told them the news. "Things are already bad enough between us and the Westerners, and this isn't going to help any."

"It's like stealing," White Deer protested gently.

"And it'll only make them madder, right?" Spinner asked the others.

Bull started to gloat. "Who cares? The white demons have been cheating us ever since we came here. They stole my uncle's gold claim, and when he complained, they killed him. Twenty Chinese saw it, but they couldn't convict the killer because only white people could testify in courts back then. And we're still getting raw deals everywhere. We always have to do more work for less money. It's about time someone stuck up for us."

"But the Westerners are miners just like us," Father said. "We have the same problems, so we should be working together to solve them."

Mr. Spenser hadn't understood the exchange, but he pointed at Father and then the other Chinese who had gathered in the tunnel by now. *"In fact, have all the Chinamen switch rooms with the Americans."*

"I don't think that's such a good idea," Mr. Eagleton said in a

low voice. *"Feeling's running high."*

Mr. Spenser glared at Mr. Eagleton. *"It's high time everyone in this mine realized that I'm the boss. I say who digs where."* As he stalked off, Mr. Eagleton followed, trying to get Mr. Spenser to change his mind. He could see trouble ahead just the way we could.

CHAPTER | 12

Michael Purdy
Rock Springs
Monday, June 15
Late afternoon

I remember when Pa first bought us the house and moved us here. He was a small man who liked guns almost as big as him. I'd heard tell that he was richer than the kings of Babylon. Whenever I saw him, he always was tricked out in the fanciest rigs and came loaded with presents. It was always sunshine when he visited.

He liked to hunt and had come west to collect antelope, deer, and elk heads to put on his wall. That was how he had first met Ma, because she'd helped out in the boardinghouse where Pa had been staying.

Every time we saw him, he promised to do the right thing soon. That alibi had worn thin over the years, like a cheap shirt that had been scraped over a scrub board one too many times.

Ma never gave up hope and had drawn all the things Pa'd

promised on the walls. Then two years ago Ma got the letter that said Pa was dead. She cried and cried. I didn't figure a person had that much water in them. But when the tank was empty, she'd gotten up and done a new load of wash.

I went around to the back, where Ma was. I wanted her to hop at Miss Virginia's clothes right away, but Ma's face went hard as a scrub board. "That woman. Nothing's clean enough for her. Well, we've got other customers too. So Miss Holiness will have to wait her turn. Oh, and be sure you get something on her account."

It was her own quiet little way of protesting. However, it was me who was going to be hit with the insults, not Ma.

I just sighed. I guess I owed it to her.

That afternoon, when I made my deliveries, the air was even hotter and stiller and enough to make a body itch right out of his skin. Every step kicked up dust that clogged my throat and nose. As soon as I could, I would light out for someplace wet. Maybe Oregon or California. Anyplace but here.

I left Mrs. Cranley's for almost the last because I hated to stick my nose into her neighborhood. It wasn't much more than a bunch of rickety shacks near Bitter Creek. Some of the poorer folks didn't even have shacks but lived in holes they had dug into the creek bank and popped a few boards onto for doors and half walls and roofs. They were always the first to wash out in a flood.

In the starched-collar part of town, people like Mr.

Spenser pretended I was the ghost boy. But here even ghosts were fair game for fists and feet. And I wasn't talking about just the children. Ever since they had been laid off by the mines, there were a lot of men who were glad to pick on someone else for change.

I once made the mistake of complaining to Ma, but she took their side. "You take things too personal, Mike," she had said. "Now that the Chinese took their jobs, they got too much time on their hands—too much time to brood, too much time to drink. And you're just a handy target for their anger."

I wished they would take it out on one of the mine bosses, and not on my hide; but today at least there wasn't a soul in sight as I walked among the dugouts' chimney pipes that sprouted up from the dirt like toadstools. No brats playing. No hard-eyed men and women squatting outside the cheap huts. Instead of the usual river of voices, there was only a distant rumble, like thunder on the horizon.

Every year Mrs. Cranley made a stab at a vegetable patch outside her shack, and every year she got the same results: stubby plants that looked like old cigars—nothing I ever recognized.

When I came to the area of weeds that was Mrs. Cranley's garden, I automatically turned to go around to the back of the shack. Though Mrs. Cranley's family lived in a wobbly little hut, the Cranleys were "respectable" folk. In fact, I could not recollect ever walking through a front door of someone else's home. Not even Mrs. Reilly's or Mrs. Duval's.

Someone's old, bony milk cow was drinking out of the water barrel there. I edged around her and knocked, but no one answered. I thought about going home and trying again, but that meant hauling around the heavy load twice. So when I heard a noise, I cautiously began to move toward it. As I got closer, I could make out that it was really many voices. They sounded real riled up, so I poked my head around a corner just to peek.

Someone had rigged a crude platform out of some boards and crates, and Captain Jack was on it. He wore an old blue army coat that reached his thighs, but his sagging belly wouldn't let him button it anymore. Even so, he was standing as if he was posing for his statue, with arms folded and feet at right angles to one another.

Behind him was one of the town's two doctors, Dr. Murray, also getting ready for his own statue. In front of them were about a hundred men and women.

"Now how long are we going to take it?" Captain Jack thundered. He had a voice that could carry over a battlefield.

"Look at what they done to me!" a man shouted.

"You tell 'em, Steve," a woman shouted.

When folks got themselves worked up against the Chinese, they forgot about me. For once I could move about the streets easily.

When Steve climbed up beside Captain Jack, the plank groaned under the double weight. "I didn't complain when the Company had us drive the airways for free. And I didn't object when the Company had us dig through three feet of solid rock for nothing—even though it's usual to pay. But this was too much. The Company gave us that spot. And when I tried to stand up for our rights, they fired me."

Dr. Murray suddenly moved forward on the platform. The plank bowed like it was going to break.

He jabbed his index finger at Johnson. "How long has it been since the Chinese took your job?"

I guess Johnson was taking time off from propping up the front of Kincaid's store. "Six months," he said.

"And when's the last time you were able to put food on your table?"

"Six months," Johnson replied, and then added, "That is, when I had a table."

"And you, diGiorgio." Dr. Murray pointed at Johnson's friend. "How long has it been?"

"Three," diGiorgio said.

Dr. Murray picked out a half dozen others and got answers ranging from two months to eight. Then he closed his fingers into a fist and shook it. "So how much longer are you going to let those Chinese take the food from your children's mouths?

Captain Jack clapped a hand on Dr. Murray's shoulder and pulled him back. "You hungry, boy?" He jerked his head at a small boy who came to school off and on. I think his name was Aaron.

"Yeah," Aaron said.

"And you, girl?" Captain Jack asked a girl of about ten.

"Of course," the girl said.

Captain Jack spread his arms. "Are we going to let our families go on starving?"

The men commenced to shouting, "No, no!" I could hear the frustration in their voices—like starved dogs yanking at their ropes.

Captain Jack stretched his arms out wide. "What's the union done for you?"

"The Knights of Labor have done nothing," Johnson hollered back.

"It's time we took our destiny back into our own hands." Captain Jack raised his fists high over his head. "It's time to take America back for Americans. It's time for all of us to be Patriots!"

A roar went up from the crowd. It was kind of exciting listening to Captain Jack. The men and women suddenly looked happy, and the children were hopping up and down.

I started to jump around with them too until I thought of Joseph. Even though we had a truce only for Star Rock, it meant big trouble for him. So it didn't seem right somehow.

Finally Captain Jack smacked a fist into a palm. "I say we don't lay down anymore. I say all Patriots should unite. That's what we'll call ourselves. Together we will whip the Company and drive out those Chinese."

"We can hold our heads up again!" Steve shouted, punching the air. "I say it's America for Americans."

There were huzzahs and cheers. With a start I saw Ma, Mrs. Reilly, and Mrs. Duval at the rear of the crowd. Mrs. Reilly and Mrs. Duval were looking happier than I'd ever seen them. Ma, though, was looking sad.

Captain Jack opened his coat and pulled out a sheet of paper and a pencil. "So sign up for the Patriotic Defense Committee. If you can't sign your name, make your X."

Men and women surged forward. Even the children tried to squeeze in. Only Ma hung back. Mrs. Reilly was tugging at her arm. "What are you waiting for, Mary?"

"What do you think that gasbag's going to do? He's just reliving his old glories from the Civil War," Ma said, sniffing.

"But we've got to do something," Mrs. Duval argued. "You're always complaining about the Chinese."

"But I don't think Captain Jack is the answer. Do you think the mining company's going to hang its head just 'cause he barks at them?" Ma demanded. "What good's a strike? When the first miners tried that fourteen years ago, the Company fired the lot of them and brought in a new pack of miners. And when that new bunch went on strike themselves, they brought in the Chinese." Ma gave a snort. "So even if you got the Company to fire the Chinese, they wouldn't hire any of these folks back. They'd just replace them with other cheap workers. Or they'd close the mines altogether."

Mrs. Duval lifted her head as if she reckoned she had Ma. "They'd lose money."

Ma shook her head. "They've got businesses all over the country. Do you think they want their workers to get ideas? Better to lose money here than lose control of the company. And it's all very well for that Steve to talk about America being for Americans; but he's Lankie, from Lancashire in England."

"You've got to have hope, Mary," Mrs. Reilly said quietly.

Ma stiffened. "I just don't go in the direction the windbags are blowing."

"Well, the doctor's no windbag. He's a learned man," Mrs. Reilly argued.

"He just wants to get him a cushy job with the territorial government. The Knights couldn't get one for him, so he figures the Patriots will," Ma said. "From what I've read in the papers, if I have a quarrel with anyone, it's with Jay Gould and the Company stockholders. There's only twelve of them, and they're also all on the railroad board. They're the ones making everyone suffer, just so they can get rich. The Chinese are trying to feed their families just like us."

"How you talk, Mary! Are you forgetting who's your own kind?" Mrs. Duval demanded.

Mrs. Reilly didn't take Ma's words any kinder. The pair of them stalked angrily toward the mob surrounding Captain Jack and Steve.

Ma saw me and frowned. "What are you doing here?"

I held up the basket. "I was looking for Mrs. Cranley." I finally caught sight of her. She was at Captain Jack's elbow, helping him.

"I'll give it to her," Ma said, holding out her hands. "You go home. I don't want you seeing any more of this."

"Why?"

Ma leaned close to my ear and dropped her voice low. "Because I've seen mobs before. They're one step away from becoming Judge Lynch. People can't take the law into their own hands. Who decides what's fair?" she asked, and answered her own question. "It's the same people who decide who's respectable and who isn't."

"Just like we're not," I mumbled.

"Today it's the Chinese they want to drive out," Ma said. "Maybe tomorrow it'll be us. I know the folks here are riled up because they're so frustrated, but they'll take that anger out on anyone who's different."

Suddenly I was scared, so I spun around, hoping that Ma was wrong but knowing she wasn't.

CHAPTER | 13

Joseph Young
Chinese Camp
Monday, June 15
Dusk

Most of the Western miners quit after a few hours that day because the railroad still didn't need that much coal, but Father was worried about our lazy cousins, so he stayed. And all the other guests had someone like our cousins too, so they also stayed and dug.

It was bad enough to have to work the extra time; but Father's decision meant I might be late for Miss Virginia's class in English.

When we got back to our camp, I couldn't wait to wash up. However, as the youngest and the lowest in the group, I had to wait my turn. I put away all our heavy gear instead.

It was warm, and the others did not dry themselves but simply went bare chested while they read the letters that had come with the supply wagon. Those who could read to those who couldn't.

Only Father washed underneath his shirt without removing it. He was always self-conscious about the scars crisscrossing his back; but as careful as he tried to be, you could always catch a glimpse of them.

Bull was lounging outside while he waited to dry; and an idle Bull was a Bull who was looking for trouble. "Hey, Otter. Where did you get those marks?" he demanded.

Father shrugged. "It's none of your business."

"Only slaves have scars like that," Bull said, "after they've been whipped."

The shirt cloth clung to Father's damp skin. "Well, you're right in one way about the slavery. I got them when I worked on the railroad."

"How?" Bull demanded.

"I'd rather not talk about it," Father said, and stepped inside the cabin to read his mail and also get away from Bull's questions,

Bull jerked his head at me. "Say, bamboo head. What happened to your father on the railroad?"

By the time I got to the wash water, it was all scummy and gray, and I was in a mood as foul as Bull's. "You know as much as I do."

"He probably stole something," Bull snorted, and he strolled away to find someone else to bother.

I opened my mouth to defend Father, but I was late

enough for class as it was. Instead I did my best to rid myself of the coal mine and wished that there had also been time to wash my hair; but it took too long to dry.

In the meantime the most wonderful smells began to float from the cabin, where White Deer was cooking our dinner; and my stomach began to remind me that it had been a long time since my last meal.

Right at that moment Ah Koon made the mistake of oozing his way into camp. He always looked ready to go to a banquet, with the crown of his head freshly shaved and his queue washed and neatly braided. Despite the heat he was wearing his expensive fur coat.

I'd seen his type before in Chinatown. They slid through trouble as easily as fish in water. He was the eyes and ears for Ah Say, who had hired us for the Company agent, Kincaid.

"Now what's this I hear about a little trouble?" he called out loudly.

The others surrounded him immediately, telling him the Company had to bring in troops to protect us.

Ah Koon gave us an oily smile. "Big grown men like you getting upset over a few dirty looks. Aren't you ashamed?"

"They're burning down Chinatowns and killing Chinese all over America," Bull said. "And the way the white demons look at us, they're probably planning to do the same thing here."

"But they won't," Ah Koon assured him, smooth as oil. "We work for Mr. Gould; and he's the richest man in America. The riffraff wouldn't dare hurt us." Mr. Gould owned not only the coal mines here but the railroad that used the coal as well as a lot of other things in America.

I left the two of them arguing outside to go into the cabin and get my carpetbag. Father was inside, snipping away at a sheet of paper. The open letter lay beside him on the bunk.

"What's the news from Three Willows?" I asked, afraid our cousins needed even more money; but it was from my grandparents. Though my grandfather had been a Lau, and the Laus were deadly enemies of the Young clan, he had become a Young himself when he had fallen in love with my grandmother.

"Your grandmother and grandfather say hello," he said.

It was hard to be friendly to people whom I'd never seen, but I tried to be polite, "Say hello to them for me."

"It wouldn't hurt to write them," he said.

I didn't want to start a quarrel, because I wanted to leave. "All right," I said as I opened my bag.

White Deer was at the stove cooking our rice. As it steamed, it cooked the sausages and dried oysters and salted vegetables as well. I wished I could stay for supper.

"What kind of good Buddhist eats sausage?" I teased.

"One who wants to keep up his strength." White Deer smiled gently.

From my bag I took my American suit. Father had told me to leave it when we left San Francisco, but I couldn't give it up any more than I could have given up my skin. It was my American badge—though I have to admit that my suit was more tight and confining than formal Chinese robes would have been.

I'd rather be uncomfortable than a fossil like these guests. With each piece of American clothes that I put on, I separated myself even further from Bull and his kind.

Though I would be hot inside my American frock coat, I deliberately pulled it on. As the last touch, I coiled my queue up and pinned it behind my head.

I studied my reflection in a mirror. With that ugly thing gone, the transformation was complete. I felt as proud and smart and modern as any American. Father could talk all he wanted to about dragon gates. Who wanted to be a dragon? I'd rather be an American like Uncle Sean. He could go anywhere and do anything he liked.

Father looked up from the butterfly he was cutting. "I don't see why you have to take English lessons. Your English is better than mine."

"Because it's nice to be able to hold a conversation in English," I said. And I would be with my own kind.

Father sighed as he went on making his cutout. "Just be careful," he said.

"I'll save you something," White Deer promised in his soft voice.

Ah Koon was gone by the time I stepped outside again. Though the sun was on the rim of the horizon, the other miners were still stripped to the waist.

Bull laughed harshly when he saw me. "Well, look at the bamboo head dressed up like a white demon." Digging a penny from his pocket, Bull tossed it at me. "Here. You want to dress up like a clown. Make me laugh."

I let it drop at my feet, instead waving to James as he left his cabin. He was a man in his twenties with a family in Canton. He was wearing a brown American suit that he had tailored himself so it fit him neatly, and on his head was a felt hat with the brim turned down in the latest style.

He raised his hat politely. *"Good evening, Joseph,"* he greeted me carefully in English.

"Good evening, James," I said with equal precision.

I felt a little flicker of pride. We were dressed in modern American fashion—not like the guests in their old, patched pants streaked with black coal dust. Why would I want to go back to a country that was full of more old relics like them?

James and I belonged to our own select club—not that Bull's small mind could comprehend that.

As we passed him, Bull made a hollow knocking sound with his tongue as he rapped the side of his head. "There go the bamboo heads."

Squirrel and the other guests began to copy him, tapping their knuckles against their heads and making the same sound.

I just kept walking. China was dead, and they were just ghosts—and they were so ignorant that they didn't even realize it.

But we were alive!

With every step, I shed more and more of bamboo head and became myself—Joseph, the American.

America was more than clothes, more than music, more than people. America was an idea, as Uncle Sean said. It was the future. And I was going to be part of it! Somewhere in America was a place where I'd be safe and where they'd treat me just like one more American. And I'd find that place someday.

We crossed the dry bed of the little creek that fed into Bitter Creek itself and then followed the train tracks southward to town.

After a couple of miles we saw Rock Springs' Chinatown on our left. The little shacks had been repaired and added onto with parts of old carts and flattened tin. We saw Paul trudging from it toward the railroad bridge that crossed Bitter Creek. He was in his thirties and had a blue suit with a checkered vest, but he didn't have James's sewing talents, so the coat and pants sagged on him. On his head he had a derby set at a rakish angle.

"*Hello,*" he said. He'd just begun English class, but he

already liked going by the American name Miss Virginia had given him. *"Hello, hello."*

"The moon is out," I said in English and began to practice my vocabulary lesson. *"We had better make haste."*

"What time is it?" James asked as we set out.

"No," I said, and tried to correct the inflection of the question. *"What time is <u>it</u>?"*

Thomas came walking from a third camp in his brown suit. *"What time is it?"* he asked in a different tone.

While James and Thomas worked on tones, Paul practiced his l's by repeating his one English word over and over as we made our way across the bridge. *"Hello, hello."*

Waiting at the other end were some more of our classmates. There were a half dozen of us who entered town, each of us in an American outfit. Theirs were donations from Miss Virginia's church; but mine had been tailored for me in San Francisco during better times.

The old guests could stick around the camps like water buffalo wallowing in mud. We were stepping into the next century.

CHAPTER | 14

Michael Purdy
Rock Springs
Monday, June 15
Dusk

I took a deep breath because delivering to Miss Virginia was like jumping off a cliff.

When I knocked on the rectory's back door, I heard the quick tattoo of shoes. The flounced curtain on the kitchen window was pulled to the side for a moment and an eye blinked at me.

To my disappointment it wasn't Miss Evie.

"Well, Michael, what a surprise," Miss Virginia said as she opened the door. "I was expecting you hours ago; and when you didn't come, I thought you were avoiding me." She glanced at the watch hanging from a chain on her blouse. "I was just about to begin the English lesson for my China boys."

"I'm sorry, ma'am." I brought the basket into the kitchen. Setting it down, I took the pile of folded clothes out and set it in a neat column on the table.

She started to examine the clothes. "When you're late like this, it makes me think you don't want my custom," she said with a hurt tone in her voice.

"I'm sorry, ma'am," I repeated. I made sure to take up my station next to the basket. If anything was missing from the kitchen, I didn't want to get blamed for it.

She crouched a little so she could examine the clothes at the bottom of the pile from eye level. "Father always says that punctuality is next to cleanliness and cleanliness is next to godliness."

I waited patiently. "Yes'm."

"Remember that next time." She smiled, straightening up.

"Yes'm. You said you wanted us to redo the last delivery," I said.

"Yes, of course. Evie wanted to do them, but I told her that it would hurt your pride if someone else corrected your mistakes." Miss Virginia nodded to a small basket near the stove.

"Yes'm." I dumped the contents into my big one; and when I remained where I was, she smiled at me, puzzled.

"Is there something else?" she asked.

I folded my hands behind my back. "If you please, ma'am, my ma asks if you wouldn't mind settling your account."

"Oh, yes, how forgetful of me," she said with a smile. "I'll have it together the next time you come."

"Just a little something maybe then," I coaxed. "There's

soap and bluing and—"

Miss Virginia glanced at her watch again. "Most of my boys are already here. We'll settle later."

"Yes'm." I sighed. Now I'd hear it from Ma when I got back. As I stepped outside, though, I thought I saw a curtain falling in another window. Was that Miss Evie's room?

I felt the puff of air as Miss Virginia shut the door behind me. As I slouched around to Front Street, an angry voice cried out, "Hey, bastard boy! I told you not to come on my street."

I did not even turn around. I recognized Seth's voice. Yesterday Joseph had been the one they were hunting. Today it was my turn. The laundry basket bumped against my belly as I skedaddled for my life.

CHAPTER | 15

Joseph Young
Rock Springs
Monday, June 15
Dusk

We all heard the shouting about the same time. Not caring about his clothes, Paul threw himself behind a rain barrel. James and the others, though, took the time to duck into a doorway.

Thomas waved to me. "Hide, Joseph." In his fear, he switched back to Chinese.

I almost took his advice. But did I really want to be cowering like a mouse?

I'd been wrong when I'd thought my classmates and I all belonged to the same club. They might think they were modern, but they were sheep like all the other guests. It was just that they could baa in English as well as in Chinese.

I'd had a lot more experience at hiding than they had, because I had been hounded by both Westerners and

Chinese in San Francisco. I could tell that the commotion was going away from us, not toward us. We weren't the target.

The last thing I wanted to do was stay with the flock. I began to stroll toward the corner like any free American would.

"Where are you going?" Paul asked in horror.

James gestured frantically. "Come back. You'll get killed."

At that moment the door jerked open behind James and the others. A Westerner with a mustache thick as a brush suddenly stood in the doorway with a fork in his hand. Around his neck was a napkin with what looked like fresh food stains. I assumed we had disturbed him at his supper. *"Play hide-and-seek somewhere else,"* he growled.

James and the other men scampered back into the street. I think the sight of an angry Westerner with a fork in his hand terrified them.

"Don't worry. If the mob chases me, I'll lead them away from you," I called. Pivoting, I went around the corner.

Once I was out of their sight, though, I stopped and checked the street. There were a half dozen ragtag boys scuffling in the dirt just before the church.

I almost retreated and waited with the others, but that would have made me just like them. And that was the whole point: I wasn't.

The boys were laughing and saying words that Miss

Virginia had never taught us. All their attention was centered on what they were doing.

My heart started to pound as a daring thought entered my mind. Why not sneak into the church school, where I could be safe?

Hugging the buildings, I began to ease my way down the street. Of course, I kept my eyes on the boys all the while. They were the same ones who had chased me on Sunday.

The big boy with the yellow hair was laughing the loudest as he kicked at something in front of him. When he shifted his feet, the movement opened a gap where I could see the target. I had thought they might be picking on some poor dog.

I was shocked to see it was Michael. He was lying on the ground clutching a basket of clothes.

There was no anger in his eyes, only sorrow. I gave a start when I realized he was resigned to what was happening. It made me feel sad and angry and puzzled all at the same time. I had to help him, but what could I do against a half dozen Westerners?

"*Take that!*" the bully shouted, and his foot filled in the gap, hiding the victim once more. I heard a fleshy thump as it made contact. It was the bullies who were making all the noise—the grunts, the pants, the shuffling of their feet, the harsh laughter. Michael didn't make a sound.

"*Leave him alone,*" I said angrily. The moment the words

left my lips, I realized my mistake.

The boys stopped and turned around slowly. And the big one sneered. *"Well, lookee here at the peacock, boys."*

"Pluck his feathers, Seth," a plump boy urged. I think he was Fred—the one with the sling.

Seth smacked a fist into a palm. *"I'll just do that, now that I'm good and warmed up."*

He came at me fast. I managed to dodge his right fist but not his left. He hit me in the eye so hard that I staggered back against the steps of the rectory.

In the end all I could do was appeal to a higher authority. I scrambled on all fours up the last few steps and straightened up. Picking up the brass knocker, I began to bang away.

It was Miss Virginia's little sister, Miss Evangeline, who came to the door. Behind her, Miss Virginia's voice floated down the hallway as she lectured. *"Your word for today is 'sanctuary.'"* She always mixed a little religion into our English lessons. *"It means a place of safety. In the old days if fugitives could reach the church, they could claim sanctuary; and after that no one could harm them."*

"Help, Miss Evangeline," I yelled, and pointed at the scuffle.

From the steps she could see the victim. She clapped a hand to her mouth. *"It's Michael."* She turned and shouted anxiously over her shoulder. *"Virginia!"*

"Now, now, Evie," Miss Virginia scolded sweetly, *"you mustn't disturb me once I've begun my class. It's not fair to my boys."*

"But this is important," Miss Evangeline said. *"There's a fight going on outside."*

Miss Virginia didn't sound the least bit concerned. *"I have more important things to do."*

"Your father—where is he?" I asked Miss Evangeline.

"He's making a call on someone who's sick," Miss Evangeline said. She lifted her head as she seemed to come to some decision, then took a parasol from a wooden cylinder by the doorway.

"The Lord helps those who help themselves," she said. *"Excuse me."* Gathering up her skirt, she headed down the steps.

Though she was smaller than me, she charged right into them, flailing away with the parasol.

"You leave Michael alone!" she said.

However, Seth snarled, *"Mind your own business,"* and with a swing of his arm, he knocked her into the dirt.

I ran down the hallway into the kitchen, which Miss Virginia used as her classroom. She smiled at me sweetly. *"How many times do I have to tell you, Joseph, there is no running allowed in our house. You must start earlier."* Then she saw my eye. *"What happened to you?"*

"They hit me," I blurted out.

"You must learn to turn the other cheek, Joseph," Miss Virginia said, and picked up our textbook. If I had, they would have blackened the other eye too. *"Where are the others who usually come with you?"*

"They're afraid to come," I said. *"Please come outside. The*

boys hit Miss Evangeline, too."

Miss Virginia gave a moan but just sat there. *"What will people think? Fighting in the street like a common little hooligan."*

Desperately I thought of the basket of clothes and took a wild guess. *"Do you know a boy called Michael? Does he bring your laundry?"*

"Yes, he does. In fact, he just picked up a load. Not that it's any of your business." Miss Virginia opened her book. *"Shall we start on page fifty-five?"*

"But those boys are going through your underwear," I lied.

"What!" Miss Virginia shot up from chair. She picked up a ruler, looked at it, and discarded it for a cane.

I barely got of her way as she shot like a cannonball toward the front door.

CHAPTER | 16

Michael Purdy
Rock Springs
Monday, June 15
Evening

At first, as I lay on the ground, I'd wished and wished I was a real ghost. Then their fists and feet would have gone right through me.

I almost didn't recognize Joseph when I saw him because he was duded up real slick. And then I wished I was dead when Seth called me a bastard. Now he knew too.

But then Miss Virginia charged in like a runaway locomotive. There weren't many beatings a body could enjoy; but this was one of them because Miss Virginia taught Seth a few things about making someone howl. She played him and his bunch like they were fiddles trying to bust their strings. She spun quick as a top as she struck out; and every blow was true.

"Are you all right?" I asked, helping Miss Evie up.

Miss Evie was more worried about me than herself. "You're

hurt. Come inside, Michael, and I'll tend to you."

I had an inkling, though, of what Miss Virginia would say if she saw Miss Evie nursing the bastard boy. "Thank you kindly, but I'd best be going."

I hurried to grab the basket and slunk away. Nobody paid me any mind. Bruises and all, I was still the ghost boy—the one everyone wished would stop haunting the town.

Like Ma had said: A bastard, a Chinese—it didn't matter to the bullies. They just wanted anyone who was different. Anyone who couldn't fight back. Joseph and I were both targets; but now that he knew what I was, would he make me a target too?

I was right glad when I got home—even if the garden Ma had drawn on the front was fading. The flowers behind the picket fence looked like ghosts in jail.

I was so worried about Joseph, I almost headed through the front door; but I caught myself in time before I made that mistake again. What if I tracked dirt on the floor? The last thing Ma needed was more work.

I couldn't use my own front door. With a sigh, I went around back. I swore that when I had a house, I was going to have six front doors, and go in and out of each one for an hour every day just for my pleasure.

But right now all I could do was worry about what Joseph was going to do this Sunday.

CHAPTER | 17

Joseph Young
Chinese Camp
Monday, June 15
Evening

Though class was only an hour long, it seemed to take forever. Usually I enjoyed the chance to practice my English, but I kept wondering about Michael. The beating had been as vicious as anything a Chinese would have gotten. What had he done to be hated so by his own kind?

I was still trying to puzzling over things when the whistles began blowing at the mines and Miss Virginia paused in mid lecture. Miners in the town and in the camps all over would be listening just as hard as we were in the classroom.

Each mine had its own distinctive whistle that let the miners know if they had to come the next day. Number Six's was high and shrill, and I heard it only faintly at this distance.

It really didn't matter for the Chinese who would be digging every day; but the Westerners would be there tomorrow because the company wanted coal. Otherwise they would stay home. However, Miss Virginia glanced at her watch. *"It's time for the class to end. I will see you next week, boys."*

We all quickstepped through the town. Fortunately, Paul and the others had come in after me, and I was glad we could travel together.

When we got to camp, we found everyone outside because of the heat inside the cabins.

"You're hurt," Father said, worried, when he saw me. He had a gentle heart. He was still the same dedicated, kind man as ever. He couldn't help it if the world had turned savage and no longer wanted him.

I winced as his finger brushed my black eye. "It's nothing."

James had to shove his oar in. "There was a mob of boys ahead of us, so we hid, but Joseph went on anyway."

Father frowned. "That was reckless, boy."

"They weren't after us," I explained. "They were aiming for some Western boy."

"Well, if they were after him, how did you get hit?" Father asked.

I had to think fast because I didn't want to tell them Michael was my friend. "I tried to stop the beating."

"That was a courageous thing to do." Father sighed.

"But I wish you hadn't risked it."

Bull turned in a slow circle as he jabbed a finger at me. "You see? You see? It's not safe in town for us anymore. Soon they'll be coming to the camps. We can't depend on the Company to protect us. We have to do it on our own."

"You m-m-mean fight back?" Squirrel asked.

Father shook his head. "If you fight back, you're more likely to get yourself killed."

White Deer chimed in, raising his soft voice so he could be heard in the group. "Otter's right. If the Westerners do come, don't resist. They just want us to leave the territory. It's better than getting ourselves killed."

"Sure, stand there and let them massacre us," Bull argued.

"Matching them threat for threat is suicide," Father said. "We're eight thousand miles from home."

"That's just what I'd expect from a slave." Bull snorted. "When they whipped you, they broke your spirit."

Father's face turned red. "Which tree survives the storm? The willow that bends or the oak that tries to fight the wind?" he asked gently.

Spinner dug his hand into his pocket and took out the paper cutout of the carp. "You're gutless, Fish Man. I don't want my son to have anything to do with you or your ideas, right?" He slapped it back into Father's palm. "Here, give it to your own son, the Fish Boy."

Father went right on trying to talk peace to the others

despite all their insults. He'd never change.

I wheeled around because I couldn't bear the humiliation anymore and went inside to find the meal White Deer had saved for me.

I had to get away from the guests who made fun of us. I had to get away from the Fish Man. Most of all I had to get away from the Fish Boy. I'd go to Star Rock this Sunday.

CHAPTER | 18

Michael Purdy
Rock Springs
Tuesday, June 16
Afternoon

The next day I was about as miserable as a body could be. At least Mrs. Reilly was ashamed when she saw me. "I'm sorry about Seth."

"Yes'm," I murmured.

From the pocket of her apron she took out a molasses cookie. "Here." She always tried to do some little thing to make up for what her son had done.

I never turned down a sweet, even if it had lint on it. "Thanks," I said, taking the peace offering. Mrs. Reilly really wasn't such a bad sort; but her son had done the damage.

When she went into the kitchen, I could hear her start on Ma right away. "If you want to get rid of the Chinese, you should come to the meetings, Mary."

"I have even less love for them than you do, Emma," Ma said. "But if we're going to get rid of the Chinese, do it in a lawful way, not like a pack of yapping hounds. We could boycott their businesses."

"A boycott isn't going to work," Mrs. Reilly insisted. "When you get a varmint in the house, you kick it out."

"A varmint, yes," Ma said, "but these are human beings."

"If you aren't the contrariest person." Mrs. Reilly sighed. "On the one hand you're always complaining about the Chinese, but you won't do anything about them."

"I know, I know," Ma said. "I exasperate myself sometimes. But the Bible makes it pretty plain you're not supposed to use violence no matter how much you think your enemy deserves it."

Of course, that set off Mrs. Reilly into quoting plenty of places from the Bible where the righteous had done just that.

I should have been listening harder to them; but I kept fretting about this Sunday. Would Joseph even show up now? Or would he copy Seth and his bully boys and shun me?

I wanted Sunday to come in the worst way—and yet I didn't.

CHAPTER | 19

Joseph Young
Mine Number Six
Thursday, June 18
Morning

I was still trying to figure out what was wrong with Michael when the trouble began.

"You stole my coal!" a Westerner shouted from the tunnel.

Father and I stepped outside to see the largest Westerner I had ever seen wave a hammer angrily over his head at Bull.

Bull didn't understand what he was saying, but he knew what the gesture meant. He raised a wicked-looking tamping needle—a tool we used for stuffing the powder charges into a hole. "This is my coal!" In his excitement he was using Chinese, which the Westerner did not understand.

In the dim tunnel the lamps cast harsh shadows on their faces, making them into the frightful masks of demons as they yelled at each other incomprehensibly.

Coal got stolen by one group or the other often enough. Sometimes it was Chinese accusing Westerners. Sometimes it was Westerners accusing Chinese.

Naturally Father waded into the middle of it, trying to straighten out the matter. "He doesn't know Chinese, Bull. Let me interpret."

"Shut up, Fish Man," Bull snapped. Spinner's nickname for Father had caught on in the camp—and unfortunately so had mine, Fish Boy. "You'll just mess it up." And Bull jabbed the tamping needle at the Westerner. "You understand this, don't you, demon?"

Squirrel leveled his drill like a lance. "Help B-b-bull!" he shouted.

From rooms all around the tunnel, Chinese came with pickaxes, needles, and drills. As he flailed his tools to clear a space through the crowd, the Westerner retreated. When Bull raised his arms, a roar went up from the other Chinese. The guests began to celebrate as if they had won a great victory.

Kneeling in the dust, I tried to shut out the angry noise. I tried to remember Star Rock and the peace I always felt there. But that seemed so far away.

CHAPTER | 20

Michael Purdy
Rock Springs
Sunday, June 21
Late morning

All the town could talk about Friday and Saturday was the theft. Throughout the day as I made my deliveries, I heard Captain Jack give the same speech a half dozen times at different spots. He seemed to be everywhere stoking up the fire and getting the pot boiling. At one rally in the afternoon, he commenced his usual way. "Are you going to let the Chinese just steal our country? When are you going to be men?"

"And women!" Mrs. Reilly corrected him snippy like.

Captain Jack bowed. "Madame, I wish I'd had a dozen of you in my company. We'd have ended the war two years earlier."

I just slunk away.

As soon as I could on Sunday, I scooted out of town. It was going to be a real sizzler—worse than last Sunday—so

I was sure that Seth and his bully boys wouldn't be out in the open countryside. They'd stick to whatever shade they could find in town—with their tongues hanging out and panting like dogs.

When I passed by the scrubby bushes, I heard a rattle in the leaves. I gave a jump. Then I simmered down. It was probably some rodent, or even a snake seeking the cool shadows.

All the craziness had made feel edgy. My feet wanted to turn back for home. Even if Ma loaded me down with chores, I'd be safe there.

I reminded myself about Joseph, though, and Star Rock. They were the one thing that let me forget my troubles. What kind of low-down skunk would crawfish right now? If I turned tail, I really did deserve all the mean things folks said about me.

So I plowed on across the hard-baked dirt past the sagebrush and the greasewood. The grit filled my nose and mouth. I could taste the land. My body badly wanted the water in the old wooden canteen that banged against my hip. I glanced at the sun. Not for another hour. Nurse my water along and I could stay out the whole afternoon.

The hardtack in my pocket was solid as stone. It seemed to weigh almost as much as the hammer and chisel I had tucked in my belt. With each step they began to feel heavier, until my thighs began to ache. Even so, I didn't stop.

Somewhere a bug was making sawing noises that rasped

my ears like a file—like the bug was the Captain Jack of this wasteland. I was right glad to get to Star Rock. Joseph was already waiting inside the cave.

"Are you all right?" he asked. "That looked like a bad beating."

"I've had worse," I said. "And now you know."

"What?" he asked.

"I'm a bastard," I said, and then held my breath.

He settled back against a wall and stared at me. "Is that why the other boys hate you?"

"Yep." I exhaled slowly. "What do you Chinese think of bastards?"

"Pretty much what those boys think." He poked a finger at the wall while he thought for a long time.

Finally I nodded to him. "Well, what do you think?"

He stretched out his legs. "I'm thinking that I've been called a lot of worse names."

"What did you do?" I asked.

"It was my father." He sighed. "He got us laughed out of Chinatown. My father thought this one proposed law was unjust. He put his faith in the American government, and he told all the Chinese to trust it too. But the government sided with some American bullies and passed the law. Now no Chinese will listen to him."

"I'm right sorry," I said.

He pursed his lips. "And the other Chinese think I'm an even worse fool because I like American things. They call me bamboo head. Yellow on the outside and hollow inside."

"That don't seem a crime," I said indignantly.

He shrugged. "Neither is being born."

"I reckon we're a fine pair," I said, feeling relieved.

"I guess we are," he agreed.

I thought about the latest rallies. "But what's been happening in the mines? In town they're claiming Chinese stole the coal."

He shook his head. "And Americans have taken our coal. By this point it's hard to say who started it. But everybody started threatening one another, so nobody ever got a chance to work out the truth. Crazy."

"Yes, crazy," I agreed.

We didn't waste any more time palavering but set to work. It seemed natural to dig in different parts of the cave. I found some good stuff. From the grunts at the other end, I knew he had too.

I'd have a lot to sketch tonight.

Finally we paused to have something to drink.

Instead of a canteen, Joseph drank from a funny-shaped gourd. "What's in there?" I asked curiously.

"Try some," he said, and offered it to me.

I hesitated. His lips had touched it. Joseph must have read my mind, because he started to withdraw it.

I didn't want to hurt his feelings. Taking it, I sipped careful like. "It's tea," I said. And lukewarm at that.

"The crews never drink water. They always boil it first and

make tea," Joseph said, taking another swig. "That way you don't get sick. When my father worked on the railroad, the Chinese stayed healthy because they only drank tea, but the Americans got ill from the water."

"I'll stick to water," I said as I handed it back.

"Suit yourself." He shrugged. When he dug his hand into his pocket, I wondered what new treasure he had brought to show.

Instead, it was a reddish-brown sheet, as flat and almost as thick as paper. "It looks like jerky," I said.

"It is. Chinese jerky." Joseph waved it at me, encouraging me to take it.

It had the same leathery feel as American beef jerky—except it was sticky rather than grainy with salt. I tore off a strip and handed it back, but waited until Joseph picked off his own strip and began to chew.

It wasn't as salty as the jerky I knew, but it was . . . "Sweet," I said in surprise.

Joseph's tongue shoved his mouthful over to one cheek so it bulged. "They put sugar and stuff in with the salt," he said.

I wanted more, but instead I made myself chew what was in my mouth. I learned this a long time ago: Make your pleasures last, because they don't come often. So before I took another piece, I'd chew what I had until I had sucked out all the juices.

"Here. Have a hardtack." I slipped my hand into my pocket but felt the other fossils I had found. I had been fooled by the weight and the hardness. "Wrong pocket," I laughed. From the other pocket I pulled out two pieces of hardtack, offering one to Joseph. "But don't blame me if you lose a tooth."

Joseph hesitated but took one. This time it was his turn to watch as I worked at a corner with my teeth. Then he did the same.

I drank a mouthful of water to help me chew the pulpy jerky and softening hardtack. He had some of his tea.

Perhaps it was some trick of the air in the cave, but I thought I heard something faint in the distance. "It almost sounds like something's roaring far away."

I'd never had much to share, not even fancies. And if I had any, I'd never have told it to Ma. Right away I was sorry that I had said that much.

Joseph, however, did not make fun of me.

"I can hear it too," he said, just as excited as me. "It's like the sound of surf."

I was impressed. "You've been to the ocean?" I asked.

"I was born in San Francisco," he said—like he missed it a lot.

"Well, how can we hear the ocean all the way from here?" I wondered.

"It's the ghost sea," he said. "It's the sea that used to be here but got all dried up."

"The lost sea," I murmured. "This is probably as close as I'll ever come to a real ocean." I sighed. "If I lived near the water, I'd go there every day."

"Maybe you could," he said sadly. "But it got too risky for us. There were drifters who hung out by the beach."

So they had bullies in San Francisco too.

Yes, but it was still San Francisco.

I picked up a pebble from the floor of the cave and chucked it outside, listening to it rattle against some other one. "If I lived in San Francisco, I'd never leave."

"I didn't want to either," Joseph said.

When we were finished with lunch, I glanced at the fossils surrounding us. "I bet those professor types got these by the bushel," I said.

Joseph stared at all the critters gleaming in the candle-light. "Can you imagine: to get paid for finding stuff like this?"

I could taste a little grit in my mouth. "It means a lot of digging."

"Better than coal." Joseph dusted one sleeve, and his shirt, though clean, gave off a faint whiff of coal. "I can never get rid of the smell. It's in my hair, my ears, my nose."

"You're turning into a fossil yourself," I teased.

He just grinned. "As long as I can shine." He motioned to one of the golden shells.

"I reckon I wouldn't mind either," I said. It was the first time I'd ever had a body to talk to about things, and it felt good.

When we both lay on our backs for a rest, the shells

shone like stars overhead; and for a moment I felt like I was floating on an ancient ocean staring up at the night sky.

What had that lost sea been like? The biggest body of water I knew was the creek when it was in flood. It was hard to think that there was anything bigger than that.

So I just closed my eyes and tried to picture nothing but water. No mountains. No town. No bullies.

Just me and Joseph drifting under the stars on a lost sea.

CHAPTER | 21

Joseph Young
Star Rock
Sunday, June 28
Late morning

Michael was waiting at Star Rock the next Sunday, as we had agreed. As soon as I slid inside, he asked me if I knew the outside as well as the inside.

"Mostly I've been in here digging," I had to confess.

"Then let me show you my secret place," Michael said. *"You might know the guts of this place, but I reckon I know the skin better."*

He led me outside the cave to a deep gully that run-off must have carved in Star Rock's side. The steep walls of the gash were nearly vertical, and we could only walk single file along the floor.

"Wouldn't want to get caught here after a cloudburst," Michael said. *"We'd drown for sure."*

However, the risk only added spice to the afternoon, and we continued along the gully. Here the air was still but cool because of the shadows.

Michael led the way, but I was the one who saw the first treasure.

"What's that?" I asked, pointing at a spot on the right wall about six feet above our heads. It looked like a round black boulder with odd knobs as big as my head.

Michael studied the swell of stone. *"It's huge."*

We scrambled up the slanted wall, making slow progress despite energetic tries. For every two feet we climbed, we slid back a foot; and each slide raised more dust and sent more pebbles cascading to the gully floor.

Finally, though, we reached the object, and I rapped it with a knuckle. *"It's some kind of stone."*

Michael joined me, caressing it in wonder and awe. *"Let's see what it is."*

I got out my hammer and chisel from the sack. *"Sure."*

I worked with light taps, chipping away a little bit of stone each time because I didn't want to damage the object. I didn't have to suggest the same method to Michael. He wanted to be just as careful.

As a result, even with both of us digging, it took a while to free more of the object. We freed about a yard of it before I finally realized what it was. *"It's a huge bone."*

Michael eyed the rest of the rock wall. *"And no end in sight. Like that book said, the minerals take the place of the bone."*

Here they had turned it the color of ebony. And the wind and grit had polished the exposed end smooth as marble.

"*In San Francisco the herbalists in Chinatown sell dragon bones.*" Suddenly I felt sorry I had rapped it. It didn't seem very respectful if it was a dragon.

Michael's hand swept along its curves. "*Or maybe this is a dinosaur. But dinosaur or dragon, I wish I could have seen it alive.*"

"*And this was just part of it,*" I said. "*I wonder how far back it goes in the mountain.*"

Michael probed with his hammer and chisel, sand and pebbles falling in a miniature landslide, until he had exposed another patch of bone. "*There's only one way to find out.*"

However, he'd had to cut deeper into the gully wall.

I caught the wrist of his hammer hand. "*Stop that. I think the bone's stuck deep in the wall.*"

He jerked his hand free. "*So we'll just go farther into the wall. Scared of hard work?*"

I grabbed his chisel. "*I've worked in the mines, so I know about the rock in this area. If you dig any deeper, you could trigger a landslide. What you need to do is widen this whole gully.*"

"*Who're you tell me what to do?*" Michael demanded angrily. "*You Chinese are so pushy.*"

"*You Americans have been bullying us for years,*" I snapped.

Michael scratched the back of his head. "*Hang it all, this peace treaty is a tricky thing.*"

I felt my own indignation change to sadness, just like the minerals that replaced bone. "*Isn't it?*"

Pebbles trickled down upon my hand, and I jerked it up

as a lizard slithered above us.

"At least we can talk about things here." He looked in the direction of town. *"It's not like outside."*

No, it wasn't.

I saw a fossil shell a yard below us. *"That's like one of those in the cave."* I thought of dragons who dwelled in the sea.

Michael indicated the level of the dinosaur bone. *"Or maybe the sea dried up and this is a land dinosaur."*

I started to slide and stopped myself by clinging to the bone. *"This is too big for my collection."* I grinned. *"It's yours."*

It was a poor joke, but Michael was eager for an excuse to laugh. *"I'd love to see Ma's face when she found it sitting in our parlor. She'd have a conniption fit."*

"Then we'll let it keep on resting here." I caressed the dragon.

Michael gazed at it. *"Maybe things don't change. The dinosaurs probably used to get just as mad at one another when they got hungry. Just like humans."*

"It doesn't matter much now," I said. And in a million years people wouldn't care who dug the coal either.

After that we talked about ourselves. He was just as curious about my life and family as I was about his.

"Your family's been here a lot longer than some of the American miners," he said.

And I told him about our camp and cabin and where they were; but he was more interested in my old life in San Francisco's Chinatown. I didn't tell him any more about my problems with Father. However, I think he left out the bad stuff in his own life too. When he told me about his home in town, he called it the ghost house.

"Ghost house?" I asked.

"There's the ghosts of all these flowers on the outside." He shrugged. *"And inside there's the ghosts of all this furniture and stuff."*

"What do you mean?" I wondered.

"I was just making a joke," he said, though his voice was sad. *"We had all these plans for what we were going to do to the house, so we sketched them in."*

"What happened?"

"They didn't work out," he said, almost biting out the words.

I waited for him to explain more, but he just looked away sadly. So I didn't push him. Star Rock was supposed to be our escape from the outside. And that might mean leaving the awful things behind us.

It was easier moving down the gully wall than climbing it. About halfway down, we found an odd fossil of a kind I had never seen before. It looked like a cone.

By the time we reached the gully floor, we'd found several more layers. Michael leaned his head back as far as he could to look up at the gully sides. *"It's just layer after layer, century after century like the books say. . . ."* He turned in a slow circle. *"When I stand here, all the fussing and feuding seem awfully petty."*

It helped put the feud between the Chinese and Western

miners into perspective. *"Whoever's right, whoever's wrong, the fight isn't between you and me,"* I said.

Michael looked down. *"No,"* he agreed.

We stood in silence, watching a hawk climb into the sky in a lonely spiral. No one to tell things to. No one to listen. Once I was like that hawk. But not anymore.

CHAPTER | 22

Michael Purdy
Rock Springs
Friday, July 3
Afternoon

N o matter how hard times got that week in town, all I had to do was think of Star Rock and I felt peaceful. I hugged that secret tight against me so no one could see, because I had to. Whenever someone like me gets something good, everybody seems to want to take it away.

So the looks and the insults and the kicks just bounced right off me; but then Miss Evie commenced to prying.

She pounced on me when I came into the kitchen with her family's laundry. "Are you coming to the July Fourth picnic? There's going to be fireworks and real ice cream."

I'd had ice cream only one other time, and it had tasted like it came straight from the Heavenly host's banquet. And I loved fireworks so much that my chest ached with wanting to go. But then I recollected what her sister had said. In fact,

I recollected it nearly every day. No one would want me. "I think I've got to work that day."

Miss Evie stared at me in amazement. "You're not going to celebrate your country's birthday?"

My cheeks must have looked redder than tomatoes, because she made me feel like the worst traitor. "No'm. It being summer and all, we've got a pile of laundry."

"It could wait for a few hours," Miss Evie urged. "You and your mother would be more than welcome."

"It's very kind of you to say," I said, setting the basket down. "Howsomever, I don't think I can go."

Miss Evie could add up two and two. "What are you scared of? The bullies won't touch you there. I won't let them."

"It's not the bullies," I mumbled.

Miss Evie jingled some coins in her hand while she studied me. "Then it's someone else."

"You just have a good time, Miss Evie," I said, holding out my palm.

She commenced to counting the coins into my hand but paused. "It's my sister, isn't it?"

I shifted my feet uneasily. "I didn't say that."

Her eyes twinkled. "You don't have to." She leaned forward so close, I got a real good whiff of the Florida water on her. "I'll tell you a secret. Even my father's scared of my sister. She talks sweet as a saint; but did you ever notice how she always gets her way?"

"A mite," I said cautiously.

Miss Evie placed the rest of the coins in my palm and closed my fingers over them. "But not this time. Promise me you'll come."

"Why?" I asked. "Because you feel sorry for me?"

"Well, if you aren't the biggest fool, Michael Purdy," she huffed. "You've got a brain and you're not afraid to use it."

When my jaw dropped, I must have looked anything but smart. "Me?"

She fiddled with her sleeve. "You're the only one I can talk to about some things."

Every ounce of me wanted to go when she said that; but I had to think of her. "I'd get you into trouble."

Miss Evie snapped her fingers. "Pshaw. I don't care."

I shook my head. She had no idea what it was like to have a whole town look down on you. "You should. This is a small town."

She sniffed. "And don't I know it. It's worse than a . . . than a . . . corset."

"Miss Evie." I looked at her scandalized. I'd washed my share of ladies' unmentionables, but proper folks didn't mention them by their specific tags. And her a preacher's daughter and all.

She was smiling with her own daring. "Well, I don't. You don't know what it's like to be a girl. You can't scratch. You can't spit. *You* try being an angel. Everyone acts like I'm not even human." She rolled her eyes. "Mother even hung little curtains on the piano legs because she thought they were too 'provocative.'"

"How could furniture legs be that way?" I asked, stowing the coins away.

"She thought they were carved too muscular . . . too masculine," she said, trying to explain, and then shrugged. "My mother finds a lot of things too suggestive. That's all she thinks about."

"I'm not sure I want to know all this about your family," I said, hunting desperately for the basket of dirty clothes.

She dragged it out from under the kitchen table. "Don't you ever feel trapped here?"

All the time. I allowed as how I did sometimes and quickly added, "But most folks do, I reckon."

Miss Evie lifted her head triumphantly, as if she had made her point. "So why do we have to do what everyone expects? Come to the picnic."

Almost every part of me wanted to say yes, but there was a small patch that was sane. "It just wouldn't be wise, Miss Evie."

"Don't be a coward," Miss Evie challenged me.

Miss Evie was the only one in town who had a kind word for me. She lent me books and gave me some school supplies and other things. I couldn't let her tarnish her name even if she wanted to. Miss Evie might have a ton of book learning, but she didn't know much about real life.

"You have fun for both of us," I said, and left.

It seemed like I was always running away.

CHAPTER | 23

Joseph Young
Chinese Camp
Saturday, July 4
Evening

I listened to the fireworks going off, but when I went outside, I couldn't see them.

I wasn't aware I had company until I heard a knuckle rapping on a skull. "Why don't you go into town and join your American friends?" a deep voice asked.

I whirled around to see Bull sitting outside.

"Some other time," I said, turning back in the direction of town. I wondered if Michael was out celebrating the birthday of our country.

Bull sighed. "I just don't understand you, boy. You want to be an American even when they hate you."

I thought of Uncle Sean and of Michael. "They don't all hate me," I said, craning my neck to see something in the darkness.

Bull laughed softly. "This is the way it's always going to

be for you, boy: watching from a distance."

I shook my head. "Being an American is more than skin color."

"You said my kind of China doesn't exist anymore," Bull growled. "Well, I say your kind of America doesn't either. There's no place for you to go, boy."

I didn't say anything as I heard him get up and go inside. From behind me, I could hear our cabinmates begin to laugh. I wondered if he had told them of my latest stupidity.

I stayed outside long after the booming had stopped and the fireworks had ended, staring at the darkness and wondering where there would be a home for me.

CHAPTER | 24

Michael Purdy
Rock Springs
Saturday, July 4
Evening

It tore me up inside something fierce to hear the fireworks.

"Come out here, Mike," Ma called to me from outside.
"You're missing them." *Boom.* "Oh," she said, "that was the
prettiest yet."

I kept thinking over and over what Miss Evie had said:
We were trapped. I guess all mice knew when they were
caught.

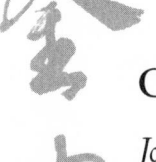

CHAPTER | 25

That Sunday Michael had been in a funny mood. Eventually I suggested moving from the caves up to the dinosaur bones. I thought the change of view might do him some good; but Michael still hardly said a word, just stared at the fossils in the rock walls.

Finally he patted one of them. *"Do you reckon the dinosaurs killed one another off like we humans are doing?"*

"I guess some of them did," I said. *"But others probably got along just like we do."*

He thought about that a little. *"But how did these fellows wind up here? What if they floated right into a trap. I mean one so tight that they couldn't even breathe. Like being in a . . . a corset. And then they just died."*

I looked away, mildly embarrassed by the mention of underwear. *"I suppose. What put that into your head?"*

"A friend," he said, tapping at the bone.

Which meant he had double the friends that I did. *"I don't know how much choice the dinosaurs had."* Certainly no more than we did.

Michael turned, looking at the wasteland around us. *"We've got to get out of here soon."*

I thought over what Bull had said. *"Maybe you can. But I'm not so sure I can."*

"What about San Francisco?" he asked.

I shrugged. *"I've read the newspapers. San Francisco sounds like it's just about as bad as Rock Springs these days. I could be just trading one trap for another."*

He scratched the back of his neck. *"I never thought about that. I just figured I wouldn't tell folks in the next place I was a bastard. But what if someone from Rock Springs came along?"*

"And how would you make a living?" I asked. I didn't want to live on Uncle Sean's charity; but how would I earn my keep? There were no coal mines in San Francisco even if I had wanted to dig for that stuff anymore.

"I only know but the one thing," he said, rubbing his rough, red hands together.

I twisted around to gaze at the bones. *"Are we going to wind up like the dinosaurs too?"*

"I hope not," he said, but suddenly his voice didn't carry much conviction.

CHAPTER | 26

T here's some questions that get under your collar and itch worse than burrs. And Miss Evie's and Joseph's were that kind. I was so busy thinking that I knocked over a bucket of water.

Ma straightened up from the washtub. "Honestly, where is your head today, Mike?"

"Sorry, Ma," I said, heading for the mop. "I got a botheration."

She blew a stray strand of hair from her mouth. "Like what?"

I just stood there with my hand on the mop shaft, wondering whether I should tell her or not. I just *had* to talk to someone. "Well, what would you do if you were a mouse and you had your tail caught in a trap?"

"Get out of it, of course"—Ma laughed—"even if I had

to chaw off the end of my tail."

"But what if there are traps all around?" I asked.

"Land, but you seem set on killing off that imaginary mouse of yours." Ma rubbed the small of her back. "Then that mouse has only two choices: Curl up and die or find a way out."

"But how?" I wondered.

"Well, how should I know?" Ma shrugged. "It's your mouse. But if that critter's smart enough, it'll find a way."

CHAPTER | 27

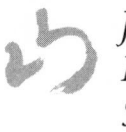

Joseph Young
Rock Springs
Sunday, July 12
Morning

That Sunday we just naturally wound up back at the dinosaur gully. As I patted one of the big bones, I said, *"I wish some of the skull were exposed too. I'd like to know what it looked like."*

Michael hesitated and then drew a notebook from his sack. *"This is one of my pa's, but I don't recognize any of the bones here."*

He held it in both hands as if it were a treasure. I took it and opened it carefully. On the inside cover Michael had written out his address neatly. At first the pages didn't make sense, until I saw the pictures. *"They're big bones."*

"Well, they're not exactly like these bones." Michael reached over and turned the pages to a picture of a giant lizardlike animal. *"Anyway, this is what a dinosaur might have looked like."*

"It's like coming on a train wreck," I said. *"You keep finding odd*

bits and pieces, but you don't know the stories behind them."

Michael patted the bone. *"I'd sure like to know."*

He sounded just as frustrated as me. *"Maybe we'll find out someday,"* I said. *"But how did your father know all this?"*

"He was a real college man," Michael said. *"But he liked to hunt. First it was wild game, and then it was dinosaur bones."*

"College," I said wistfully. *"I bet the professors could tell us."*

Michael stared down at the journal. *"That's it! I've been hunting and hunting for a way out, and it was plain as the nose on my face."*

"What is?" I asked, curious.

"The way out of the trap," he bubbled.

I stared at Michael. *"What are you going to do?"*

He slapped the bone so hard that the sound echoed between the walls. *"I'll go to college. Maybe even Pa's college."*

"Really?" I asked.

He saw the doubt in my face. *"I know it sounds crazy."*

Wild as the notion seemed, I tried to encourage him. *"But if you could, you'd get so many answers."*

He lifted his head as if he were gathering steam again. *"If I could, I'd be out of here."* He waved a hand toward the wasteland.

"But how?" I asked.

He scratched his head sheepishly. *"First you figure out the answer. Then you figure out the way. I don't know how yet, but I'll come up with something."*

I felt like I'd been inside a dark box and never known it

until someone ripped off the lid to let in the light. I bet Uncle Sean would help. Of course, even if he could, I didn't know if a school would take me; but it seemed worth trying. *"I'll go too."*

He stuck out his hand with a grin. *"Then let's go to the same one together."*

I took his hand and shook it solemnly. *"That's a promise."*

CHAPTER | 28

Michael Purdy
Rock Springs
Monday, July 20
Afternoon

I didn't sleep much Sunday night because I was too excited about our plans. I knew it was sort of farfetched. But if you don't shoot at the target, you can't hit it.

That meant I was a little tired the next day. By the late afternoon I was just shuffling around and yawning. So I was right glad to reach Kincaid's Mercantile, because that was the last of the day's deliveries. I was just setting out the clean aprons when Steve stormed past.

Steve hipped me out of the way. I almost stumbled into a stack of cans of beans. "I need a drink, Kincaid," he snarled, and jabbed a finger at the brown bottles on the shelf behind the counter.

Mr. Kincaid came around the counter and took the basket from me. "What's the matter, Steve? Wear out your welcome at all the other stores?"

Steve banged a grimy fist on the counter. "What do you care? My money's good." His face was unshaven and his toes were showing through one boot. He'd fallen on hard times since he'd lost his job in the mines.

Mr. Kincaid carried the basket behind the counter and set it down. "For weeks you've been telling the whole town that I'm scum because I help contract for Chinese labor."

Steve waved a hand toward the two men eavesdropping outside. "If it's okay with Johnson and diGiorgio, it's okay with me."

Mr. Kincaid straightened. "I'm the only one willing to give them credit. Is that what you're asking for too?"

Steve dug his hand into his pocket, pulling out a wrinkled dollar bill and some change. He nudged the coins around on his palm as he counted and then slapped everything onto the counter. "I'll pay you the rest."

Mr. Kincaid pulled a ledger book out from under the counter and leafed leisurely through the pages. "I don't see how I can let another person have credit. I'm already carrying a lot of families. I've got to stay in business, Steve. You understand."

Steve wiped a hand across his forehead. "Oh, I understand all right. You charge us full price for our tools; but you sell them to the Chinese at cost. I'm telling you that I've had as much as I can stand."

Mr. Kincaid slammed the book shut. "Maybe the smart ones were the ones who left town."

Steve leaned against the counter. "You'd have plenty of customers with money if the Company wasn't trying to drive all the Americans from the mines. That miserable bunch of bloodsuckers want to hire nothing but foreigners. Now how can Americans get treated like this in their own country? It's the Chinese's fault I can't even afford to get drunk. They got me fired."

"As I recall, there were two sides to that matter." Mr. Kincaid slid the book to the side. "And I wish you'd quit waving the flag. You're an Englishman, not an American."

"Well, I'll settle down and marry here as soon as I save a little money," Steve said. I wasn't sure what woman would have had him, though. "I'm not like the Chinese. They keep their families there."

"That's because we don't let them bring their wives here," Mr. Kincaid said.

"Well, you don't want them breeding," Steve argued.

"If you've got to blame somebody, blame the Company, not the Chinese," Mr. Kincaid snapped.

Steve scraped the money from the counter back into his palm. "Just whose side are you on?"

Mr. Kincaid pulled out his cash box. "I'm on the side of common sense. It's not the Chinese treating you this way. It's Jay Gould. He wants cheap coal for his railroad."

Steve curled his fingers around his money. "We could make Gould sit up and listen if it wasn't for those Chinese. You pay them a few pennies and they grow fat. You treat them worse than rats and they kiss the boot that kicked them."

I almost blurted out what Joseph had told me that first Sunday—that the Chinese were just as desperate as the American miners. However, I caught myself in time. Being a friend to a Chinese was worse than being a bastard.

Steve scowled. "If they won't take the hint, maybe it's time for the Patriots to do something more drastic."

Mr. Kincaid began to count out some coins for me. "As long as the Chinese pay their bills, they've got just as much right to be here as you."

Steve drew his finger across his throat. "Maybe it's time to get rid of those pests." He added significantly, "And their friends."

Mr. Kincaid slid the coins over to me. "Nothing good ever came of that kind of talk."

Steve jingled the coins in his fist. "Maybe it's time for more than talk."

Mr. Kincaid studied Steve for a moment. Then he took a bottle from the shelf. "Sweet dreams."

Steve hesitated and then took the bottle. "I'll pay you back soon."

"Don't ever come in here again," Mr. Kincaid said. "I won't be threatened in my own store."

Steve gripped the bottle. "Dr. Murray and Captain Jack have the hang of it."

"You stick around them and you'll hang, period," Mr. Kincaid warned.

Steve, though, had worked itself into a good hissy fit. "Us Patriots'll fix those Chinese soon. Nobody takes what's mine."

He shambled out of the store, bumping into a shelf and rattling the tin cups on it as he struggled to uncork the bottle.

Mr. Kincaid took a pencil from behind his ear and made a notation in a ledger book. He looked up when he saw I was still there. "Something else, Michael?"

"Yes, sir, but . . ." I hesitated shyly. I wasn't used to drawing attention to myself.

"But what?" Mr. Kincaid inspected the blunt point of his pencil and then began to sharpen it.

"Do . . . do you think the Patriots will do what Steve says?" I asked.

Mr. Kincaid tucked the pencil away again. "I've had this store ten years, my boy, and I've yet to hear a miner carry out one threat. Steve was just trying to get my sympathy so he could get drunk in midday."

I was still worried. "He seemed pretty worked up."

"I wouldn't pay Steve no mind, boy." Mr. Kincaid stowed the book away. "If he didn't have the Chinese to blame for his troubles, it'd be Laplanders or somebody else."

"But some of the other miners seemed just as mad," I said.

Mr. Kincaid laughed. "This is 1885, boy, not the Dark Ages. You don't slaughter people wholesale."

I thought of Steve's face and wondered. But then I shook it off, because nothing that happened in town mattered. The only thing that counted was Star Rock. And I'd be right glad to get there.

CHAPTER | 29

Joseph Young
Mine Number Six
Tuesday, July 21
Before sunrise

In San Francisco's Chinatown I had seen the sky only in strips—and the city lights dulled the stars—so I'd never paid much attention to the sky. In Wyoming, though, Heaven had taken a whole bucket of stars and splashed them across the sky.

The sun hadn't risen yet, so the stars were little pinpricks in the purple dome of the sky. And on the ground the lanterns on our caps bobbed up and down in answer as we made our way from the camp to the mine. All around me the miners coughed and spat. I knew if I could see their spittle, it would be black from the coal dust.

We couldn't move very fast because of our load of tools—shovels and hammers and picks and drills and other gear.

Even more than other days, I wished I could have

stayed in camp. The day before, some Chinese over in Room Twelve had grabbed the wrong cart. By the time they noticed their mistake, they had filled it with coal. When the Westerners came to get their cart, the Chinese promised to give it back once they had unloaded the cart. But the Westerners tried to take the cart with Room Twelve's coal. There would have been a terrible underground battle if Mr. Eagleton had not come along and sided with the Chinese.

Bull had gotten puffed up over the "victory." He bragged about it all that day and last night, and was still boasting this morning about the lesson we had taught the Westerners.

I tried to ignore Bull, concentrating instead on the small circle of light cast by my lamp and wishing I could be at Star Rock with Michael, free from all the bickering. It would be nice to talk with my friend about something pleasant.

Bull's boasts and the threat of violence sickened a good man like White Deer. "Fighting solves nothing," he scolded gently.

"If you d-d-on't like it here, why don't you go to San Francisco then?" Squirrel asked sullenly.

"I'd be there fast as an arrow if I could find work," White Deer said in a soft, wistful voice. "I heard from a friend a while ago. There were so many Chinese who have fled there that there were three people for every job. And since then there's been a lot more expulsions from the other Chinatowns, so I bet San Francisco's is even more crowded. The odds must be even worse now at finding something."

I hated to see White Deer so sad. Of all the crew, he seemed too tenderhearted for this rough way of life.

Father's light jerked up and down as he nodded his head at White Deer. "Well, I have some classmates with businesses in San Francisco. I could ask one of them to hire you."

"You went to school together, Otter?" White Deer asked.

"No, we worked on the railroad in the same crew," Father explained. Back in China anyone who passes the government exams is a "classmate."

White Deer nodded. "From what I hear, the railroad would have been tougher than any other exam."

Father rubbed his chin. "Let's see. One of them owns a restaurant and another owns a theater. But I just got a letter from Bright Star. He's working at a laundry, so I could see if there's another job. Why don't I write him tonight?"

That cheered up White Deer a little. "Tell him I'll take anything, even if it's just sweeping the floors."

As we rode the pit cars down into the mines, I wished I could go to San Francisco with him. And we weren't an hour into work before I would have left, job or no job.

When I saw a redheaded Westerner by our cart, I asked, "Can I help you?"

When he straightened up, I saw he had an armload of coal.

"*That's our coal,*" I said, climbing through the room's doorway to him.

"*I'm just taking back what you stole,*" he said angrily.

"*We never took anything from you,*" I protested.

The Westerner laughed. "*You want it? Here!*"

I ducked the first lump of coal, but the second was one as big as my fist and it caught me in the stomach, so I went down with a shout.

"What's wrong?" Bull came out of the room. "Get away from him," he warned the Westerner in Chinese. The Westerner ignored him and began to throw coal at Bull.

Raising his shovel, Bull charged. The Westerner kept hitting him with coal, but the lumps might just as well have been flowers for all the effect they had.

The Westerner dropped the rest of the coal and began to back down the tunnel. Bull, though, caught up with him. He kept swinging the shovel, and the Westerner kept dodging.

Father and the other crews came out into the tunnel. "Are you all right, boy?"

I could feel the bruise on my belly, but otherwise I was fine. "I guess."

"I'll be right back," Father said to me, and then headed

for Bull and the Westerner. *"Stop that,"* he said in Chinese, and repeated himself in English.

Then I could hear Mr. Eagleton roaring, *"What's all the hooraw?"* He strode through the crew and toward the two men fighting.

He and Father got Bull and the Westerner separated. *"Now what's this all about, Jake?"* Mr. Eagleton demanded of the Westerner.

"It was just a misunderstanding," Jake said.

Bull looked at Father for a translation, but I spoke up before he could. *"I caught that American stealing,"* I said.

"Did you, Jake?" Mr. Eagleton demanded.

"No, sir," Jake insisted.

"He's lying," I said as I walked toward them.

Jake looked as if he wished he had thrown something bigger at me. *"The boy misunderstood. It's just like yesterday."*

Mr. Eagleton turned to me. *"What happened, Joseph?"*

"I caught him taking coal from our cart." I pointed at the floor. *"You can see it on the floor. He started throwing it at me."*

Mr. Eagleton folded his arms as he looked back at Jake. *"You've cost the Company enough time."*

"Are you going to take his word over mine?" Jake asked, outraged.

"All you've done is cause trouble ever since I hired you. Just like your friend Steve," Mr. Eagleton said. *"This is the straw that broke the camel's back. You're fired."*

"But I got a wife and a kid. The kid's sick," Jake protested.

"You should've thought of them before," Mr. Eagleton said. *"Now come with me and we'll settle up."*

Jake turned to the rest of us. *"Steve tried to warn me. He told me you'd destroy us one by one unless we stand together."* When the other miners remained silent, Jake swore at Mr. Eagleton. *"It ain't going to end here."* And then he whirled and shouted at us. *"It ain't going to end here."*

His words echoed defiantly in the tunnel.

CHAPTER | 30

Michael Purdy
Rock Springs
Sunday, July 26
Morning

The heat made my clothes stick to me like a second skin. Ma hated this kind of weather, so I wasn't surprised when I found her still in bed. "Are you all right?" I asked her.

"No, but I got loads to do," she said. "When the air gets damp like this, everyone sweats and needs clean clothes."

I was afraid she'd rope me into working. "It's Sunday, Ma. Even the Lord rested today."

"The Lord didn't have to answer to Miss Virginia," Ma said, but she stayed in bed. "This heat just saps all my energy."

"Take a holiday," I urged. "You earned it."

I made tea and porridge and brought them to her. Ma didn't stir. "Just set them down on the floor. I'll eat later," she said, and rolled over.

I felt a little guilty; but before Ma could stick me with

work, I got my hammer, chisel, and provisions and dumped them all into a gunnysack I'd found. With that over my shoulder, I headed toward Star Rock.

Miss Evie, though, was outside the church, sweeping. "Coming to church today, Michael?"

"I reckon not," I said, dipping my head apologetically.

She was so busy looking at me that she didn't see her broom wasn't touching the steps as she moved it. "I missed you at the picnic."

"I . . . I warned you I was busy," I said. "I'm sorry."

"I was pretty mad at you," she allowed, "but you're the only one who understands what I'm going through. I guess I have to forgive you."

"I'm right glad of that," I said truthfully. I hesitated and then asked, "Miss Evie, did you ever stop to think what you'll do after you finish school here?"

Miss Evie leaned on her broom. "I don't know," she admitted. "Maybe start teaching myself."

"Why not college?" I asked.

She drew her eyebrows together real thoughtful. "I hear there are some schools back east for young ladies." Then she shook her head. "But my family would never agree."

I threw her own words back at her. "So you'll stay in the trap?"

She gave a start. "But it's impossible."

No more impossible than my plans, so I told her what I was telling myself. "Well, why not try? At least you'll have something to aim at."

Miss Evie began to whisk the broom back and forth quickly while she pondered that, and then stopped. "You do have a wild side after all."

"I just never had the right target before." I grinned.

Miss Evie laughed mischievously. "Well, since you're taking chances, come to church today. Father will be grateful for anyone at his service. Most everyone in town's at the big rally."

"For what?" I asked.

Miss Evie shook her head, disgusted. "Getting rid of the Chinese. Sometimes I think you and I are the only sane ones in town."

It was hard to turn down an invitation from Miss Evie, but I had promised Joseph. "Maybe some other time."

"Did my sister say something to you?" Miss Evie asked.

"No'm," I lied. I didn't want her to get in trouble with Miss Virginia.

"Don't be scared of her. I can talk to my father," Miss Evie said.

"Please don't," I said. No one won against Miss Virginia. She'd find ways to pay back both Miss Evie and me.

She looked sad as I began to back away. I guess she judged I was crawfishing again. "Well, maybe next Sunday."

"Maybe," I said, and hurried away.

The Patriots' rally was so big that they had to hold it on the edge of the town. Everyone but Ma and Miss Evie's family must have turned out for it.

For the occasion someone had even built a real platform for the speakers. It was covered all over with red-white-and-blue bunting. And on top of it was the usual gang of suspects: Captain Jack trying to drum up his own army, Steve getting revenge, Dr. Murray nailing down an easy government job.

"How long are we going to take it?" Captain Jack was shouting from the platform. "This is our country."

Like a ghost, I skirted around the edge of the big crowd.

"And anyone who tries to speak up gets fired." Captain Jack put his arm around Steve. "Like this man."

"I ain't the only one." Steve waved at someone in the crowd. "Come up here, Jake. Why don't you do something more than complain?"

Jake was a redheaded man who climbed up beside Steve. "Steve warned us things would only get worse if we didn't do something about the Chinese." He turned and shook Steve's hand. "And he was right. I crawled on my belly enough. I'm a man, not a snake!"

Steve beamed as he slapped the redheaded man on the back. "Welcome to the cause, Jake."

Captain Jack wasn't going to let anyone else steal his thunder. "Who else will stand up? It's time to show those Chinese what we're made of. And if they won't listen to words, we'll let this do the talking." From his waist he pulled out a gun. "I say we burn Chinatown and the camps down, and they leave either on their feet or in a box. And I say we do it now!"

I stared in shock.

"Who's with the Patriots?" he yelled to the crowd.

There was a roar and a forest of arms shot up, punching fists at the air.

Suddenly a familiar voice demanded from behind me, "Where are you going, bastard?"

Because I'd been heading to Star Rock, I'd gotten sloppy at being a ghost and let Seth and his bully boys sneak up and catch me.

"For a walk," I said.

"We ain't seen you much," Seth said.

"I didn't think you wanted to see me," I said, wishing immediately that I had kept my mouth shut.

Seth slammed his fist into his hand. "We got to make up for lost time."

I did my best to look surprised. "You want to beat me up instead of getting to the free eats?"

"Free eats?" Seth asked uncertainly.

"They're over there," I pointed. "They got cake and doughnuts and cookies and everything. But with this mob they ain't going to last long." Then I took out a piece of hardtack and shoved it into my mouth before they could see what it really was.

That tore up Seth something fierce—feasting or bullying. His belly won out in the end though.

"Watch him while we check," Seth ordered Fred.

Then the rest of them commenced to worm their way through the crowd while my guard glared at me, mad that he was missing all the food.

Somehow I managed to mumble around the hardtack. "It's going to be all gone by the time you get your turn."

Fred shifted from one foot to the other. In the old days he'd ignored me; but then his pa got laid off and took to drinking. Fred had started to show up at school with bruises and such; and after that he'd hooked up with Seth. Even so, his kicks and punches had always been halfhearted, so I reckoned I could work on him because I could see he was caught between his fear of Seth and his hunger.

"It's not like I was going away from town forever. You can always beat me up tomorrow," I said. Too bad that was true.

"If you're not here when I get back, you're going to get it even worse tomorrow," he warned, and he hightailed it after them.

I tried not to think about the next day as I headed out of town.

Miss Evie was right. Nowadays most everyone seemed crazy except for me and her.

Even away from the town I could hear the shouting. Only it didn't sound like people anymore: It was like they were becoming one big monster, all riled up and wanting to get even.

On the horizon I saw a dark, angry smudge. Rain was going to come soon.

I started to run toward Star Rock. Not only did I want to get to the cave before the showers, but I also wanted to get away from the monster, away from everything, back to the peace and calm.

Joseph wasn't in the cave, so I sat down to wait and try to work my way around the hardtack with the help of the water. But my problem was even harder to swallow. At Star Rock we weren't supposed to talk about what happened in town or at the mine. But I didn't see how I could keep them away from here anymore.

I had finally forced both down my throat when I heard his footsteps. As soon as he was halfway through the entrance, I blurted out, "Did you know there're talking about burning down Chinatown and the camps?"

Joseph paused at the cave mouth. "The American miners make threats every day now. My father says the Company will call in soldiers like they did when the Chinese first came here."

I scooted back to give him room to come in. "They sound like they're finally ready to stop talking and actually do something. There's a rally outside town, and they're waving guns."

Joseph crawled in and settled heavily against a wall. "Guns?"

I jumped when light suddenly flickered across the opening.

"It's just lightning," Joseph said. A moment later we heard a huge boom of thunder.

The storm had begun.

CHAPTER | 31

Joseph Young
Chinese Camp
Sunday, July 26
Late morning

As soon as Michael told me about the guns, I knew Father had made his biggest blunder yet. We'd jumped from the boiling water straight into the fire by coming here.

I glanced at the cave opening at the outside world, but the rain was like a dark curtain. Even so, I felt scared, as if an armed mob were lurking right outside.

The last thing I wanted to do was go out there. I just wanted to stay in Star Rock, where it was safe.

But Father was still at camp; and even if the others insulted me, I couldn't let them die either.

"You okay?" Michael asked.

I started to gather up my things. *"I've got to warn the camp."*

Michael grabbed my shoulder. *"The mob won't attack in the rain."*

"*If it were your mother in the camp, would you stay here?*" I asked.

He sank his head back. "*At least wait until the thunder and lightning are over.*"

However, I was already on all fours. "*I can't. We need to send word to the other camps as well.*"

"*But you could get hit by lightning,*" he protested.

Sometimes all you can do is laugh. "*It's just a question whether the mob or the lightning gets me first.*"

He slid out of my way. "*Good luck.*"

"*Hope you find lots of good things,*" I said as I began to crawl back toward the mouth.

He crossed his legs. "*I don't feel much like hunting either. Think I'll just wait out the rain and go home.*"

When I crept outside, the rain lashed my face like a whip of needles. I almost scurried back, but lives were depending on me.

I tried to straighten up—and nearly got bowled over when the wind slammed into me like a giant hand, trying to toss me against Star Rock. With the rain whirling around me, I lost my sense of direction. Then I saw my tracks and started to slog through the mud, following them.

When the light flashed, I threw myself into the ooze. Of course, by the time I saw the lightning, it would have been too late if it was aimed at me. Out in the open the thunder crashed so loudly that I felt as if my head were inside a bass drum. It made me remember Miss Virginia's stories about the End of the World.

Michael had been right. The mob wouldn't attack in this weather. When the lightning was blasting everything in sight, only a crazy person would walk through it— someone as mad as Father.

I guess I was my father's son after all.

About halfway to camp, the tracks started to blend into the mud. I stumbled on in what I hoped what was the right direction, though the winds whipped the rain into my eyes so that I was almost blind.

I found the camp by dumb luck rather than by skill. Or rather the camp found me: I bumped into a wooden wall and fell backward into the mud.

Struggling to my feet, I put a hand on the cabin and used it to guide me to the street that ran down the center of the camp.

Light burned cheerily in the windows. Either the miners hadn't gone to the mines to work on their own time, or they had come back early.

I never thought our beat-up cabin would look so good. I opened the door; then a sudden gust caught it so that it banged inside.

You couldn't have asked for a more peaceful scene. Father was cutting a dragon out of paper. White Deer was preparing a meal. Squirrel was shaving the crown of Bull's head—that was the fashion that went with the queue, but a lot of miners didn't bother. Spinner was playing chess by himself—and looking as if he were losing both ways. Others were simply catching up on their sleep.

Bull looked up, irritated. "Close that door, Fish Boy. You're letting the rain in."

I was so cold, my teeth chattered and I couldn't get any words out.

"I'll throw another log in," White Deer said gently, moving toward the stove.

Father got out a towel. "Get those things off right away, or you'll catch a cold."

I stripped, leaving my clothes in a soggy puddle on the floor while Father dried me off.

"You should've headed back right away as soon as you saw the clouds," he scolded me.

As I pulled on my spare pair of pants, I tried to warn Father. "F-f-father . . ." However, I was still shivering too bad.

Father draped the towel over me like a cape. "Wait till you warm up before you try and talk."

"Here's some tea," White Deer said, bringing over a tin cup.

Though its sides were hot, I held it between both palms, glad of the heat. Then I sipped it, feeling the warmth flowing through my body and branching out into my arms and legs. I'd finished half the cup before I set it down and pulled on a shirt. Then I put the towel back around my shoulders for additional warmth.

"We have to get the Western soldiers to come," I finally said to Father.

Father gathered up my wet things. "Mr. Eagleton keeps telling us not to worry."

"But now the whole town's talking about burning down the camp and killing all of us," I said. "And they've got guns."

It was suddenly quiet in the cabin.

Father looked confused. "How do you know?"

Squirrel dropped his razor. "D-d-did you sneak in there?"

"Yes," I lied.

Bull folded his arms. "I had you pegged all wrong, Fish Boy. You've got some guts after all."

Father, though, was even more puzzled. "How did you get into town without getting caught?"

I remembered what Michael had said. "I didn't have to. The rally was outside town."

Squirrel was suddenly suspicious now. "You d-d-didn't have on your white demons' clothes, so you couldn't have been in disguise."

Too late, I realized my mistake. "What I meant to say was that I heard it from someone else."

Father was skeptical now too. "What Chinese got close to that rally?"

Bull made a disgusted gesture. "He's just full of wind like you are."

I had been trying to avoid telling them about Michael, but I saw I had no choice if I wanted them to believe my warning. "I made a friend, a Western boy. We go looking for fossils together."

The crew glanced at one another and then stared at me angrily—as if I had just stolen ten tons of coal.

"You're really done it now, Fish Boy," Bull said, and rapped a knuckle against his forehead to remind me I was hollow as bamboo.

I couldn't understand why Bull was being so hostile when I'd just been trying to protect him. "What?" I demanded.

"He's a spy. You gave him information for the attack," Bull snapped.

I almost laughed because the idea was so absurd. Their minds were closed off by a wall of suspicion—just like those of the Westerners in the town. "What secrets? All he'll learn is that we're people too."

Father shook his head. "I had no idea you were going that far away from camp. You're not to go again."

"But he's my friend," I protested. "Just like Uncle Sean is yours."

That caught Father by surprise. "That good a friend?"

"Yes," I insisted.

Father thought a moment and then sighed. "If the Westerners are carrying guns now, it's too risky to leave camp. What if those other Westerners catch you? I don't think you should go to English lessons anymore either."

For once Bull agreed with Father. "They won't stop with just a beating."

I stared around me in disbelief. Star Rock was all I had to look forward to. The thought of losing it was making me feel all crazy and wild inside. "My friend's all I have," I protested angrily. "He's the one thing that makes this place livable."

Father took a deep breath and then let it out slowly. "When you get mad at me, you look just like your mother."

That caught me by surprise. We never talked much about her. I think it hurt Father too much. But I was always hungry to know more, so I forgot to stay furious. "Did she get angry at you often?"

Father gave me a crooked smile. "More than I like to remember."

"Like what?" I asked.

But Father just changed the subject, as usual. "I'll go see Mr. Eagleton."

Spinner was still frightened. "There must be something else we can do, right?"

We all jumped when the light flashed through the window. For a moment I thought it was the flash from a gun muzzle; but then we heard the boom of thunder, rolling through the camp.

In the sudden silence, I heard White Deer praying over and over in a soft monotone. "Lord Buddha save us."

CHAPTER | 32

Michael Purdy
Rock Springs
Sunday, August 9
Afternoon

I don't know if it was just a lot of whooping or if the storm discouraged them, but the Patriots didn't attack the Chinese. I just sighed in relief that things were okay.

But when Joseph didn't show up the next Sunday at Star Rock, I got all hangdog. What if the Patriots had caught him? Then I realized that if they had, they would have been bragging about beating up a Chinese boy.

It's funny how you can miss a fellow. I should have been happy to have all the fossils to myself, but somehow it didn't seem the same. The shells didn't glitter like stars. They were just funny-shaped rocks.

I tried and tried to hear the ocean and look at the stars; but it stayed the same dusty, dark hole. I reckon the magic wasn't in Star Rock. It was in us; and it took both of us for it to work.

It was the same with my dreams. Somehow college didn't mean the same without Joseph. So finally I just gave up and slunk back home.

Next Monday I hung around the church at the time that Miss Virginia gave English lessons; but though I saw the other Chinese, there was no sign of him. That really set my mind to worrying. Was he sick—or worse, had a mine collapsed on him? My imagination really started galloping like that.

The worries were just like little bugs that had gotten under my skin. The next Sunday I paced around outside the cave at Star Rock. And when he still didn't show up, I figured I'd better track him down myself.

He had told me where his camp was, but I smelled the cooking fires long before I saw it. The odor of barbecue set my stomach to rumbling and my mouth to watering.

On the edge of camp, I saw a Chinese. "Excuse me," I said. "Have you seen Joseph?"

He stared at me like I'd just dropped down from the moon.

"Joseph's my friend," I said. When he still looked puzzled, I patted my chest so he'd get the idea. "Friend, friend." And I took a step closer; but that made him take to his heels, skedaddling like a jackrabbit that had seen a coyote.

I was wondering if maybe I shouldn't hightail it out of there myself; but I couldn't face another day of fretting over my friend, so I plodded on.

Ahead of me I could hear the man shouting excitedly in

Chinese. What if they came after me with picks and drills?

I just hoped Joseph was around to keep me from becoming a porcupine. Still, I slowed down careful like.

The buildings in the camp were not real different from the little shacks in the poorer part of Rock Springs. The man was standing there hollering and pointing at me.

"Excuse me," I called, but that made him only yell louder.

Doors started to slam open, and the Chinese started to pour out. I couldn't believe how many were jammed into each cabin.

I almost lost my nerve right then, but I didn't see any weapons.

I held up my empty hands to show them I was harmless. "Easy now. I'm just here looking for my friend, Joseph."

The crowd just stared at me like chickens watching a hawk. Finally another man stepped forward. He had a book in his hand with his index finger saving his place. "What do you want with him?" he asked in English.

I felt relieved to find someone I could talk to. "I just want to be sure he's okay." There was something familiar about his face though. I could see Joseph's nose and cheeks and ears. "Are you Joseph's father?"

"Yes," Mr. Young said. "Now you'd better go before there's trouble."

His warning was already too late, because the biggest Chinese I ever saw muscled his way through the crowd. I didn't understand what he said to me until he used one

English word. "Go, go," Mr. Muscles kept shouting, but all I could do was stare at the pickax in his hand.

Mr. Young started to argue with Mr. Muscles, who began to get redder and redder. Just before Mr. Muscles turned into a beet, Mr. Young waved at me urgently. "You'd better leave."

At that moment, Joseph popped out of his cabin. A Chinese man followed, trying to yank him back inside. However, Joseph pulled free.

"Michael," he called.

He seemed just as glad to see me as I was to see him. Suddenly I forgot about Mr. Muscles and all the other Chinese.

"I've been waiting and waiting for you at Star Rock," I said. "Where've you been?"

"My father won't let me go. He thinks it's too dangerous to go there," Joseph explained.

I'd heard enough talk around the town to know his father might be right. "Well," I offered, "I could come here and study and make plans."

I think Joseph missed me as much as I did him, because he turned to his father. Though he used Chinese, I could hear the hopeful tone.

Mr. Young hesitated, but he didn't say no outright.

However, Mr. Muscles raised his pickax over his head and charged toward me. "Go, go, go."

Joseph leaped on one arm, but it was like trying to pull down a thick tree branch. Mr. Muscles was starting to aim at me despite Joseph's weight. All around him the other Chinese were backing away.

Mr. Young stepped in front of me and held out his hands. Mr. Muscles shouted angrily, but Joseph's father stood his ground. He had more guts than I did.

"Please go," Mr. Young said without looking at me.

Over his shoulder, I could see Mr. Muscles's face. It had the same wild, crazy look as Captain Jack's.

I didn't wait for any more. I lit it out of there like a deer with its tail on fire.

CHAPTER | 33

Joseph Young
Chinese Camp
August 9
Afternoon

As Michael ran away, I let go of Bull. "Are you crazy?" I asked.

Father shoved in. "You can't bully some poor boy. That's just the kind of excuse the Western hotheads need to tear this camp apart."

Bull leaned on his pickax. "Then we'll show them how sharp our picks are, Fish Man." He turned to his ring of admirers. "Are you with me?"

And the idiots actually started to cheer. Bull turned slowly, basking in their approval. Then he jerked his head at Father. "We only put up with you because you can speak that weird demon tongue. But that doesn't make you the boss."

Now that the danger was over, Squirrel crowded in and patted Father on the shoulder. "Yes, you b-b-behave yourself, Fish Man, and do what we say. And we'll protect you."

Father pulled away angrily. "That kind of 'protection' will get us all killed."

White Deer tried to make peace. "They're just boys. What's the harm if they get together here?"

Bull towered over White Deer. "We're at war now. Spies can come in all sizes and ages."

In the crowd I saw James from my English class. "Tell them. There are good Westerners too. We can trust them."

Bull tilted back his head and announced in a loud voice, "Anyone who sides with the demons is a traitor to all Chinese."

James glanced at Bull as if he were afraid. He didn't object. He just slapped his sides helplessly. Even White Deer was intimidated.

Squirrel narrowed his eyes. "You b-b-betrayed us once in San Francisco. Are you going to let your son do it here?"

Father looked around at the rest of the camp. There wasn't one friendly face. The few who weren't angry at us were like James—too scared to say anything.

Father had taken so many unpopular stands that the last thing I expected was for him to back down; but he let his breath out slowly, like the air going out of a sack. Then he faced round to me again. "What if your friend has some accident here? Let's say he falls down and gets a bruise. The town could claim we did it and burn our camp down. Things are like a powder keg right now."

Bull nodded smugly. "Now you're finally thinking, Fish Man. That could be the match that sets off an explosion."

Father rubbed the back of his neck, embarrassed. "In a little while, when things calm down, you can invite him, but not now."

"If there's any traitor here, it's you," I said. "I've stuck by you in all our troubles; but this is how you repay me."

I could see the muscles working around Father's jaws as he fought to control himself. "I'm sorry, boy."

As the truth slowly dawned on me, I felt like he'd just taken his pickax and swung the point into my side. "All you think about are your causes and the family back in China. You don't care about me at all." I'd been only fooling myself to think he loved me.

Bull was puffing himself up, savoring his triumph. "Your father's finally showing some common sense. It's high time you did too, Fish Boy."

I turned slowly, staring at each of them. "You're dinosaurs! And fossilized dinosaurs at that. With rock-hard skulls and stone for brains."

Squirrel nudged me. "L-l-like should stay with like. Never forget you're Chinese, Fish Boy."

And it was just like they had shoved a big trap up against me and the jaws had snapped shut over my leg. "The guests in San Francisco told me to stay with my own kind. And now you're telling me here. But all you do is call me Fish Boy. I hate it and I hate you!"

"If you hate Chinese, you hate yourself, you bamboo head," Bull said, and rapped a knuckle against his forehead.

"I'm not Chinese," I snapped. "I'm as American as Michael."

Bull thrust out an arm so I could see his brown skin. "This says you're Chinese." And he pointed to his eyes. "And this." And then he held up his queue. "And this."

I couldn't do anything about my skin or my eyes, but I could do something about my queue. "I hate this thing," I said. "The Manchus make us wear this as a sign we're their slaves." And I ran into the cabin. White Deer's cooking knives were in a box where they always were, and I snatched one up.

"Calm down, boy," Father said from the doorway.

Bull and Squirrel had followed Father into the cabin. "He's threatening to kill himself," Squirrel announced to the others.

I had no such intention; but they all looked afraid. Suddenly I had a feeling of power. No wonder Bull liked to brandish his pickax.

Even Bull looked worried. "Don't do anything stupid."

"I'm an *American*," I insisted, holding up the knife.

"Yes, certainly," Father said gently as he took a step forward. "We'll work things out. Just be patient."

I could feel my hand shaking with anger. "I'm not your kind of Chinese, Father, and I'm not Bull's. I'm my own. I don't care if you think that makes me a traitor."

"Of course," Father agreed, taking another step. "Now put down the knife. You don't want to hurt yourself, Precious Light."

That was the last straw. I felt the anger explode inside me, blowing away any hesitations. "It's not Precious Light and it's not Fish Boy," I screamed. "It's Joseph!" And with my free hand, I grabbed my queue and held it up while I brought the knife around behind me.

I saw the horror in all their eyes as they finally realized what my real goal was.

"Stop that. You don't know what you're doing," Father said, and started to run forward.

I backed away.

"You don't want to do that. The knife might slip."

Bull grabbed Father. "I think he means it."

"I do," I said, and sawed away at the queue.

Father stopped dead in his tracks, but he held out his hands. "If you cut that off, you can't go back to China. The Manchus would kill you as soon as you got off the boat."

Thank Heaven that White Deer kept his knives sharp. Just a bit more and I'd be free. "I'm never going to China."

"But you're Chinese," Squirrel said.

"You don't have to go to China to be Chinese," I said, hacking away. "You can be a Chinese in America."

"But they don't want Chinese here," Bull said.

"Then I'll hold on like a barnacle. They won't ever get rid of me," I said. I felt the knife cut through the last strands, and I held up the rope of hair in triumph. "I'm free."

Father sat down on a bunk. Squirrel slumped on the floor and just stared in astonishment. Bull shook his head. "What a pair you are. Fish Man wants to be the demons' lapdog, and Fish Boy wants to be an actual demon."

Opening the stove, I threw my queue inside. "I'm here to stay."

Squirrel watched as the burning queue began to coil like a living thing upon the coal. "You just condemned yourself to die here."

"A demon fool for a demon grave," Bull grunted.

PART TWO

CHAPTER | 34

Michael Purdy
Rock Springs
Sunday, August 30
Late morning

Every Sunday for the rest of that month I waited for Joseph at Star Rock, but I saw neither hide nor hair of him.

I hadn't known him long, but I didn't have to. From almost the very beginning, I had known we were alike; and now I felt like I'd lost half of me.

I tried to take some notes on the bones and fossils in the cave, but it didn't seem the same anymore without him. I needed his excitement and encouragement.

He never poked his nose in town either; but I can't say as I blame him. Tempers began truly boiling after the railroad laid off Americans and brought in Chinese to take their place. The whole territory was turning ugly: In Cheyenne, Chinese got stomped. Rawlins and Laramie chucked the Chinese out altogether.

At the end of August signs popped up on walls all over town warning the Chinese to leave or else. They were signed by the Patriots.

Folks made their own improvements, painting skulls and crossbones on the signs.

Of course, there still were a lot of folk in town who thought that kind of talk was crazy. I could see it in their eyes and the way they held their mouths shut tight; but like me, they were just too scared of the Patriots to open their mouths.

Mrs. Reilly and Mrs. Duval kept pushing and prodding Ma to join, but she refused. She had too much work to do to waste on talk. I could see it bothered her something fierce, though, because she commenced scrubbing the clothes extra hard. She even tore up Mr. Kinkaid's shirt on the washboard.

She looked at the raggedy hem. "That's what I get for pretending the dirt spots're the Chinese."

I wished I could tell her what Joseph had told me: that the Chinese had it just as bad as us. But that would have opened up a whole can of worms. So I kept quiet and went out to Star Rock.

But there was just me and the old dead stars.

CHAPTER | 35

Joseph Young
Mine Number Six
Tuesday, September 1
Afternoon

A t first it was strange to feel the cool air on the back of my bare neck; but after a few hours I got used to that.

But I didn't expect everyone in camp to avoid me. In their eyes I was now worse than a fool: I was a traitor. They seemed to think I would pass on information to our enemies.

Well, dinosaurs wouldn't understand humans, would they?

The only one who had a kind word for me was White Deer; and that was only because he was so happy after receiving the letter from Uncle Bright Star, who said there was a job for our friend.

"I'm going to escape this place," White Deer said with a bow to Father. "And I owe it all to you, Otter."

I felt a little twinge of jealousy. Now that I couldn't go to Star Rock, I wanted to return to San Francisco more than ever.

It hurt that Father spoke to me only when it was about work. The rest of the time he looked puzzled whenever he saw me.

We had been so close once that now it hurt—like a cut inside that refused to heal. But I wasn't about to apologize. I realized that he was just a Chinese pretending to be a Westerner. In the end he wanted to be able to scuttle back to China like all the other dinosaurs. He didn't care at all about what I thought.

When the mine superintendent, Mr. Spenser, came to get us, Father didn't say anything. He just gestured for me to come with him and Bull and six others.

It was usual at the end of the month for Mr. Spenser to mark new rooms. This time it was in an area called Entry Five, which everyone said would be the richest location yet. So the others were feeling pretty good about the future.

The next morning, though, five of the crew weren't feeling well.

"I told you not to eat that fruit," White Deer scolded.

"Sure, sure, Mother," Squirrel grumbled. His bunk bed creaked as he rolled over on his side.

"You're going to be late," Bull warned.

"I'm too s-s-sick today," Squirrel said, and waved his

hand. "As I nap, I'll be dreaming of you slaving away in the mines."

"Dream a little for me, too," Bull said, sighing.

When we got to the mines, Mr. Spenser was sick too. Today it was Mr. Eagleton who was temporarily in charge.

Father muttered to himself, "Squirrel's going to feel even worse when he knows he's got a Western disease."

Once we were in the mines, we went to our new rooms.

When I stepped into the tunnel to take a short rest, I was surprised to hear the clink of metal from Room Two, which should have been empty today because its team was sick in our cabin. Curious, I poked my head inside.

A Western miner turned around. The coal dust mixed with the sweat on his face, and his lungs labored as he tried to breathe. He barely had the wind to ask, *"What do you want?"*

Despite the dust that masked his features, I recognized him as a man called Whitehouse. Mr. Spenser and Mr. Eagleton were always careful around this Westerner. I'd heard he was also in the government somehow—though in China, no government official would have been working the mines.

"This isn't your room," I said. *"This belongs to Chinese."*

"This is where Eagleton sent me," the miner said. *"Now git."*

I found a second Western miner working Room Four, another of the new rooms that had been assigned us. When I told that to Father, he shrugged—and coal dust spurted into the air from his shoulders. "If Mr. Eagleton told them to take those rooms, it must be okay. Mr. Spenser must have changed his mind and told Mr. Eagleton to switch the rooms."

By the afternoon Whitehouse had had it. Through the doorway to our room, I saw him trudging back up the tunnel with his tools. For all their complaints about Chinese taking their jobs, many of the Westerners did not work as hard as we did.

I didn't think anything more about it until lunch, which we took in the tunnel along with Bull and White Deer.

It was there that Father told them about the change in assignments.

"Those weasels talked their way into our rooms," Bull snapped.

"They aren't 'our' rooms," Father reminded him. "They're Mr. Eagleton's."

"Fish Man," Bull grunted, "I'm through being cheated and bullied by demons."

White Deer tried to calm Bull down. "I'm sure we can straighten that out." His voice was so soft that I wasn't sure Bull heard him. But he had.

"I'll do it myself." Setting down his lunch, Bull rose angrily.

Father grabbed Bull's arm. "This is no time to start a fight here. Who knows where it could end?"

Bull jerked free. "It's time to act like men; but you

wouldn't understand that, would you? Just crawl underneath your rock and leave this to me."

"Don't do anything rash," Father pleaded.

Knowing Bull, though, he was bound to. We were finishing lunch when he returned with some other Chinese from our camp. He stopped in his room long enough to get his gear. The others already had ours.

"What are you going to do?" Father asked.

"Claim our rooms," Bull said, holding his big pickax in his hand like a sword.

We watched as Bull entered Room Two, where Whitehouse had been working today. The others went into the rest of the empty rooms so they would all be occupied.

"Let's talk to Mr. Eagleton first," Father urged.

Bull raised his head proudly. "This is one Chinese the demons aren't driving out of the territory. It's time to take a stand." Turning, he smiled when he examined the wall. "How thoughtful. Someone's already set the charges for me."

I could see the holes driven into the wall, from which fuses dangled.

"Don't do this, Bull," Father warned.

"Step back, Fish Man, if you don't want to get blown up," Bull said.

After Bull lit the fuses, he joined us in the tunnel.

The explosion brought another Western miner to

check. *"What are you doing? This is Whitehouse's."*

Bull picked up his shovel from where it leaned against the wall. *"Go, go."*

Father grabbed the shaft of Bull's shovel. "Are you crazy?"

Bull shoved Father so hard that Father fell onto the ground. "Go back to making your paper fish, Fish Man."

In the meantime the Westerner had shouted and danced around, and when he had shouted himself hoarse, he said, *"You haven't heard the last of this."*

I helped Father to his feet. "I'll try to find Mr. Eagleton."

Father dusted off his pants. "I think it's too late for that now," he said, and shook his head. "Way too late."

CHAPTER | 36

Michael Purdy
Rock Springs
Tuesday, September 1
Evening

Ma and I were halfway through our meal when Mrs. Reilly came steaming through the back door. "You know what those thieving Chinese done now, Mary?"

Ma calmly spooned some peas onto her plate. "No, but I have an idea you're going to tell me."

Mrs. Reilly sputtered as she told us about how the Chinese had stolen Mr. Whitehouse's room. She folded her arms over her stomach indignantly. "We're holding a big meeting now to figure out just how to fix their wagon."

"The Chinese might have their own version of things," I suggested.

Ma looked disappointed at me. "Mrs. Reilly and I are having a conversation, Mike. You are not to interrupt."

"Yes'm," I said, hanging my head.

Ma cleared her throat. "But Mike has a point. Though I have no love for them, I'd like to hear their side before I'd do anything drastic."

"This is your last chance, Mary," Mrs. Reilly warned. "Show us you're one of us."

"I'm for myself. Always have been and always will be." Ma turned to me. "Pass the biscuits please, Michael."

Mrs. Reilly slapped the table in frustration, and the forks and knives rattled. "How can you eat at a time like this?"

Mrs. Reilly was now leaning between Ma and me; but Ma calmly reached around her and took the plate of biscuits from me.

"Easy. I'm hungry," Ma explained. "And eating will accomplish a powerful sight more than a lot of folks screeching like owls."

Mrs. Reilly gazed at her more puzzled than riled. "Mary, we got so many rights in the Territory that we don't have anywhere else in the country. Women can vote and hold on to property and get the same pay as a man. So you can't sit at home. You've got to fight when you see something wrong."

"I not only have the right to vote, property, and pay, I got the right to my own mind," Ma appealed. "Emma, you're my best friend. Don't follow this track. Set down with me so we can chat like the old days."

Mrs. Reilly straightened up. "I'm sorry. You've always been my best friend too, but I can never set foot in this house again."

As she stormed out, I sat back in my chair. "Ma, maybe it wouldn't hurt to go."

Ma just stared at the biscuit in her fingers. "She was always wasting my time jabbering. If she doesn't visit anymore, I'll get more work done." But suddenly she held her napkin up to her eyes.

"Ma?" I asked stupidly.

"Excuse me," she said, getting up. "I've got something in my eye."

She stumbled blindly from the kitchen. The next moment her bedroom door slammed, but through the thin boards I could hear her crying.

She was now just as lonesome as me. You would have thought two lonely people could keep each other company; but that's only if both are them are normal. And all I brought Ma was a bushelful of tears. I knew I couldn't be a comfort to her. I just sat there listening to her weeping and feeling more useless than ever.

CHAPTER | 37

Joseph Young
Mine Number Six
Wednesday, September 2
Morning

That morning when Father and I woke up, Bull and the others were already gone. "They didn't even have breakfast," White Deer said in a soft, disappointed voice.

"That's not like Bull." I shivered. The cabin's stove hadn't been able to drive away the bitter cold of the night. Anyone stranded outside would have frozen. "Usually he wolfs down twice as much as anyone."

Father was dressing hastily by the light of the kerosene light. "That's what worries me. I think they're going to do something foolish at the mine. I'll meet you there."

White Deer clanked a spoon exasperatedly against a pot. "Not you too, Otter! Aren't you going to have breakfast either?"

Father gave a little one-legged hop as he pulled on his

pants. "I'm going to talk sense into them. But you have breakfast and then bring me something."

"We might as well take breakfast for everyone," White Deer said, his usual gentle self.

"Precious Light will give you a hand," Father said. Grabbing his hat, he started for the door.

"Do you think Bull will listen?" I asked.

"I hope so," Father said, and left.

I wrapped my blanket around me against the cold and stared at the worn wooden boards while I wished I were a thousand miles away.

As White Deer filled a clean bucket with rice and salted vegetables, he glanced at me. "Why don't you and your father join me at his classmate's laundry in San Francisco?"

I shed my blanket and began to dress quickly in the freezing air. "Father won't go. People might resent having him there and make trouble for his classmate."

"I had a dream the other night," White Deer said. "The Lord Buddha came and warned me to get away from here."

"I don't need a dream to make me want to leave," I said.

Lighting my lamp, I walked through the twilight with White Deer, wishing that my pigheaded Father would join Uncle Bright Star in the city. And when the wolves began to howl, I did more than wish. I began to pray.

I began to pray even harder once I entered the tunnels. The Westerners were muttering to one another and glaring at any Chinese they saw; and the Chinese were doing the same to any Westerner. You could feel the anger hanging in the air just as black and just as explosive as a cloud of coal dust.

It was the worst I'd ever seen. My scalp and hair tingled like they did before a thunderstorm.

I knew Bull had to be in the middle of the poisonous brew, so I headed straight to the room that had caused all the trouble yesterday.

Sure enough, Father was trying to make Bull and Squirrel see reason. "It's bad enough that you set off the Westerner's charges. Don't take his coal," he was saying.

Bull gripped his pickax stubbornly. "Will you quit blabbing on and on? You'll do more good, Fish Man, if you pick up a shovel and help us."

Suddenly Whitehouse burst into the tunnel with Mr. Eagleton close on his heels. *"This is my room,"* Whitehouse thundered, his voice bouncing off the low ceiling. *"And that's my coal."*

"This my room, my room," Bull insisted just as loudly.

Mr. Eagleton tapped his chest. *"I'm the pit boss, and I say it's Whitehouse's."*

Bull wasn't budging an inch. *"Mis-tuh Spenser, he give my friend."*

It was the kind of the thing that Father had straightened out before, so he wedged in between them. *"This is all a misunderstanding. Mr. Spenser assigned the room to one of our cabin-mates without telling Mr. Eagleton, and Mr. Eagleton gave the same* room to Whitehouse without informing Mr. Spenser. We can settle this once Mr. Spenser gets here."

"That suits me." Whitehouse nodded.

However, when Father tried to explain things to Bull, the big man flung Father against a rock wall. "Are you trying to help them cheat me out of our friend's room? Get out of my way, Fish Man!"

"Father," I said, and ran over to him. As I helped him sit up, Bull and Whitehouse started to trade insults at one another. It was like watching two goats battle for a herd.

"I've got to stop them," Father said groggily.

It was already too late though. "I stay. You go," Bull yelled, and raised his pickax over his shoulder.

Whitehouse's fist shot out, catching Bull right on his chin; and the big man dropped backward onto Squirrel.

And that little misunderstanding was all it took: the match that set off the powder keg.

"H-h-help! We're being attacked," Squirrel yelled, his voice echoing down the tunnel.

And Whitehouse started shouting the same thing in English.

There had been fights between the Chinese and the Westerners before; but this time it was different. Hate drove both sides. In the dim light the warriors whirled like shadow puppets of demons; and the tunnels echoed with screams of pain and anger.

Poor Father had tried just as hard to head off trouble

here as in San Francisco, but in the end he was still help-less to stop it.

That didn't keep him from trying even now. When I saw him square his shoulders, I began to be afraid he was going to do something even more foolish.

"Hide in a room," Father ordered as he got to his feet.

"Come with me," I said, trying to grab his arm.

"I can't," he said.

I don't know where Father found the courage. He went among them, trying to break them up and shouting in both Chinese and English. "*Stop.* Stop."

I should have helped him, but the screams got to me. I hid in a room, crouching and feeling like the worst cow-ard. What good was my knowledge of American songs and clothes right now? For that matter, what good was being smart? It was all very well to want the rest of the world to be like Star Rock; but wishing wasn't going to make it happen.

I thought I was so smart because I was modern; but all I could do was hide like a coward. Maybe the world still needed old dinosaurs like Father, who would wade into a fight.

After about a half hour the noise stopped. Father's voice, though hoarse, grew softer. When I peeked out of the room, I saw a half dozen Chinese lying on the ground and about a dozen Westerners bleeding from cuts. Father had managed to separate the two groups. I don't know if it was his appeals that had done the trick. Both sides were so winded that I think they were glad of a break. *"We're going,"* he said to the Westerners.

Whitehouse leaned against the cart. He looked a little sick from the sight of all the blood. *"I think you'd better."*

"Get Bull," Father said to the others.

They improvised stretchers out of shovels and pickaxes, laying the injured people across the shafts.

Whitehouse motioned the angry Westerners to back away and form a lane. *"Let them through."*

"We won't work here as long as those Chinese thieves are around. We want the Chinese out!" someone shouted, and the other Westerners took up the chant. *"Chinese out!"*

"We should go on strike till they're gone!" another miner yelled. And the cries of *"Strike, strike"* mixed with the earlier chant.

It made me a little nervous to go past all the angry miners, but we made it to the surface without another incident.

Up there we tried to tend to the wounds. Bull was unconscious, as were several others. We were just finishing up when Ah Koon strutted up in his thick fur coat with Mr. Spenser and Mr. Eagleton.

The three of them quickly got things sorted out; and when Mr. Eagleton fetched Whitehouse and Mr. Spenser had explained things, Whitehouse looked guiltily over at Bull and the other wounded. *"All that bloodshed and for nothing."*

"A strike won't don't anyone any good," Mr. Spenser pointed

out to Whitehouse. *"Make too much trouble and the railroad will just go elsewhere for its coal, and you'll all be out of jobs. If you return to your room, maybe the others will go back to theirs."*

Whitehouse nodded. *"I'll try to talk to the others."*

As he headed down into the mines with Mr. Spenser and Mr. Eagleton, Ah Koon said to Father, "You're all such babies. Come with me." And we headed over to the Chinese miners.

The other wounded Chinese had been bandaged with strips torn from shirts—though I thought the dirty cloth might do more harm than good. Bull was moaning in pain.

White Deer knelt beside him, trying to make him comfortable. "Bull needs a doctor. He's in a lot of pain."

Father rubbed his chin. "There's only two doctors in town, both of them Western."

Squirrel spat. "And Murray won't see Chinese."

"There's Dr. Langhorn," Ah Koon said to him.

Squirrel's head shot back as if Ah Koon had tried to bite him. "G-go into town? You've got to be cr-crazy."

Ah Koon tried to calm him down. "Don't worry. We've already set up signals. If you see a red flag flying over Chinatown, that means there's trouble. So come back here."

Squirrel was too afraid of the risk, so Ah Koon was growing more and more frustrated. As he mopped the sweat from his face with a silk handkerchief, White Deer shot to his feet. "The demons are coming!"

The Chinese around us clutched their tools, tensing for another fight; but the Westerners marched right past us as they headed toward town. As they walked, they kept chanting about going on strike.

"It was all a misunderstanding," Whitehouse pleaded from behind them. *"It wasn't my room after all. He was right about Spenser."*

"Then you get the coal for Spenser," a red-bearded miner jeered. *"We ain't putting up with the Chinese no more."*

A fat miner turned, shouting threats as he walked backward. *"We're going to remember what you did, Spenser. And on top of that, you made us walk out of here."*

Mr. Spenser stopped and glowered. *"You're strikers now. I only let working men ride in the pit cars."*

I was sure that the Western miners would add that pettiness to the long list of grievances.

Exasperated, Mr. Spenser waved his hat at us. *"Well, this is your lucky day, boys. There's all the more coal for you to dig."*

However, once Father translated, the others were staying put. "Those demons are still mad. It's not safe here," Squirrel said.

One of the other miners turned. "I'm going back to our camp."

"But we have contracts," Ah Koon protested.

"They won't do any good if we're dead," Squirrel shot back, and then said to the others, "Come on. Help me carry Bull."

As Ah Koon alternated between pleading with us and trying to placate an angry Mr. Spenser, the others picked up Bull on the makeshift stretcher.

"I'll get Dr. Langhorn," Father said, "and bring him to camp."

I thought again of how I had stayed in the coal room cowering. If I wanted the rest of the world to be like Star Rock, I'd have to learn to be brave—just like Father and not like some mouse.

"You should stay with them," I said. "You need to keep them calm." I glanced around, but there were no other volunteers. I didn't want to go, but I didn't see what choice there was. "I'll fetch the doctor."

"You're coming with us," Father insisted.

"I can speak English and I know the town," I said, hating to be so logical. "I can find my way around even better than you can."

Father hesitated.

I nodded to the other Chinese who were milling around like lost, frightened sheep. "They need you."

"But I need you," Father said, putting a hand on me shoulder.

That surprised me. "You do?"

He touched the back of my neck and touched my jagged fringe of hair. "I need you more than all the causes in the world and the family back in China. As wild as you are, you're my son."

"Then I'll come back," I swore.

But somewhere in the wasteland, as if it could smell trouble, a wolf howled hungrily. And I wondered if I would keep my promise.

CHAPTER | 38

Michael Purdy
Rock Springs
Wednesday, September 2
Late morning

I was heading with a load of clean shirts for Mr. Keenan in his room in a boardinghouse. He was a gambler who liked to dude himself up. He could be almost as fussy as Miss Virginia about his clothes, but he always paid in hard coin. And a customer like that was a rarity nowadays.

Then I saw the first miners marching through town. Each of them was armed to the teeth with pistols, rifles and shotguns, knives, clubs, and hatchets.

"White men fall in," they kept shouting as they marched through town.

A bell began to sound. At first I thought it was the church's, but it was too high a sound, so it had to be the little dinger at the Labor Hall, which the Patriots must have taken over.

Seth and the other boys were drawn to the ruckus,

parading alongside the miners like pups with a big dog.

I sidled in toward the rear. "What's the fuss?" I asked one miner.

"The Chinese have gone too far this time," he said, and began to hooraw again so I waited until he stopped to take a breath.

"What mine are you from?" I asked.

"Number Six," he said.

Number Six was Joseph's.

Captain Jack came hotfooting it along the street with one arm in his coat and the other hunting for the right sleeve. "To the Hall," he hollered.

"To the Hall. White men fall in." The miner strutted off with the others.

I wished I could fly to Number Six—then I could tell Joseph what was happening here. But on foot the miners might catch me. Feeling was running high and they had guns. If they caught me talking to a Chinese, I'd get worse than a thumping.

I had gotten by this long by staying low, and I wasn't up to changing. So in the end I went on delivering laundry— but feeling bad.

By the time I finished, the miners came streaming in from Number Three and Number Five mines. Their faces were black from the coal dust, as if they had not bothered to wash before they came in. The pack of them bristled with drills and pickaxes.

I was really worried for my friend now, so I tailed the miners to the Hall. A bunch of townsfolk were standing outside, including Mrs. Reilly and Mrs. Duval, but they were too excited to notice me.

As Captain Jack told the crowd about how Whitehouse had been cheated, the hall began to mumble angrily.

Dr. Murray got up. "The time for talking is done," he announced, and grinned at the roar of approval.

For a moment there was a shoving match over who would have the lectern. When the captain started losing to the doctor, he leaned forward and yelled, "I say we meet again this afternoon. That'll give me and the steering committee a chance to come up with a plan of action. We'll show those Chinese a few tricks that General Sherman taught me."

"I second it," Steve said before the doctor could object.

"I third it," diGiorgio hollered.

They wound up voting to adjourn for now and settle the Chinese Question later.

Steve raised his hat. "And now all good Patriots to the saloons!" That cheer was the loudest of all. I stood back as the Patriots streamed out of the hall and up to Front Street, which was filled with saloons.

Fretting, I went to Mr. Keenan's boardinghouse. He was just getting up and yawned as he pulled on his silk vest. "What's all the ruckus, anyway?"

"The Patriots are meeting," I said.

He dug some money out of his pocket and paid me. "I

figured they would have talked one another to death by now."

"They got more than speeches today," I said, and I took the coins. "They got guns."

Mr. Keenan began buttoning up his vest. "Well, now. Maybe I'll mosey on over there. It'd be nice if there was some excitement in this town for a change."

Fretting even more, I headed for home. The streets were deserted—like the whole place was turning into a ghost town. Though it was safer for me than on a regular day, I felt right glad when I finally went down into our cellar. Ma was there, scrubbing away. I told her what I had seen. "Do you think the Patriots will really do something to the Chinese?"

Ma shook her head.

"Those loafers just want an excuse to drink and brag," she said. "It won't amount to cup of beans. Now hurry along with the deliveries."

I hoped Ma was right.

CHAPTER | 39

Joseph Young
Rock Springs
Wednesday, September 2
Noon

All the way into town I kept thinking over what Father had said. So he did care about me. I wished I could have talked to him more, but it hadn't been the time or the place. I wasn't sure if I would get a second chance at it. And that made me a little sad and scared at the same time.

As I passed by Chinatown, I remembered Ah Koon's warning and looked at the flagpole that rose above the roofs; but there was no red flag. Even so, now that I was close to town, I wanted to turn around right then and head back to safety.

But what about Bull? He could be dying. What would his family back in China do then? What would they do when Bull didn't come home to sit in his new house? I couldn't stand to think of their sad faces.

I might be an American-born fool, I might even be a traitor, but I wasn't going to be a coward anymore.

I knew the town well after so many trips, so I figured I'd try to slip in. There wasn't a soul in sight as I crossed the bridge over the creek.

Ahead of me were more miners straggling into town. About half of them were carrying guns; the others had hatchets, clubs, and knives. I didn't recognize them, though, so I figured they were from one of the other mines. Word must be spreading.

Something was up. I intended to warn the camp as soon as I got the doctor.

Front Street was a broad stretch filled with tracks. Saloons lined either side, but they were shut up tight, leaving a large, angry mob milling around outside.

If I was going to reach Dr. Langhorn, I would have to cross Front Street somehow. I wished I'd had time to change to my suit. With my short hair and in those clothes, they might not have noticed me.

I'd have to adopt another form of disguise, so jamming my hands into my pockets, I tried to stroll along as if I had every right to be there.

"*Get him,*" I heard a man shout.

I didn't wait to see if it was someone else. I started to run.

"*Here's ammunition!*" A Western boy clambered up on a coal car. I recognized him as Michael's tormentor.

As the boy began to throw handfuls down to the ground, a bunch of boys and men zipped in and began to pick it up and throw it. I even saw some brickbats.

"Look at him skedaddle," a miner laughed, and fired off a pistol.

I flinched but kept on running. I figured a standing target was a dead target. However, either he had missed or he had just shot into the air, because I didn't feel a thing.

"He's going even faster now," another miner hollered gleefully, and shot off his rifle.

It was only a matter of time before I fell under the storm of missiles. It's funny about moments like those. Logic doesn't really apply. I kept telling myself I had to keep my promise to my father. I didn't want to die yet.

Somehow I managed to keep my balance, and after about a hundred yards, the stones suddenly stopped. I guess the mob had gotten tired of the game.

As I reached the safety of the next street, I stopped because it hurt to breathe. I touched my left side and winced at the pain. I ached all over. Dr. Langhorn was going to have to treat me as well as Bull.

When I had got my breath back, I went on, trying to be more careful. Slipping down alleys and behind buildings, I reached the rear of Mr. Kincaid's store. He was locking up his back door.

Since he worked with Ah Say and Ah Koon, he was friendly to Chinese. *"Better take to your heels, sonny,"* he warned me. *"There's bad trouble brewing, and it's going to boil over soon. The saloons have closed. And there's nothing worse than an angry man with a thirst. The saloon keepers think they can keep the miners from getting into deviltry if they keep them sober. If you're smart, you'll head home and stay there too."*

I took a couple of steps back toward the camp; but I kept thinking about poor Bull. What if it was Father who was hurt? Wouldn't I want someone to do everything they could to fetch the doctor? So I turned around and continued on toward Dr. Langhorn's.

"Not that way, sonny," Mr. Kincaid warned.

"I have to get the doctor," I said.

"If you don't turn around, you'll be needing one yourself." Stuffing the keys into his pants pocket, he hurried off as if he were eager to follow his own advice.

As I went on, I peeked down the alleys and through the spaces between buildings. All the stores were shutting up too.

Dr. Langhorn lived in a trim little house; when I knocked at the door, a pleasant, round-faced lady answered the door. Her gray hair was piled on top of her head in a big bun.

"It's an emergency. We need Dr. Langhorn to come to our camp," I said, glancing nervously around the street.

"I'm sorry," the woman said, *"but my husband is up at Number Three mine seeing to patients there. He told me he'd be there all day."*

I'd risked the stoning for nothing, but I couldn't let

myself give in to dismay now. Bull was the important one. As long as we didn't have to enter the town where the mob was, we should be all right. *"Then we'll take our friend there. Thank you."*

I hurried away. This time I knew enough to take the long way and skirt around the mob as I headed back for Number Six.

CHAPTER | 40

Michael Purdy
Rock Springs
Wednesday, September 2
Early afternoon

Ma and I were just setting down to eat when we heard the cattywhumpus in the street; and the next lick a man was hollering, "The Patriots are calling a meeting! Meeting, everyone!"

Ma gave a snort. "Again? They just had one this morning. Folks in this town do like to jaw at one another."

I set my fork and knife down. "I ain't so hungry, Ma."

But when I started to get up, Ma snapped, "Set."

I wanted to know what Captain Jack and his committee had up their sleeves. The miners had looked mighty angry. "Maybe I ought to go see."

"Set. It doesn't signify for us," Ma insisted, and commenced grace. Just because Ma didn't go to church didn't mean she didn't believe in such things. It's just that she was even less welcome there than I was.

But as she prayed, I couldn't help thinking that ghosts didn't care what live folks did. They just wanted to stick around houses long on memories and short on everything else, fading away like the drawings of the garden and the fireplace.

CHAPTER | 41

Joseph Young
Mine Number Three
Wednesday, September 2
Afternoon

Rock Springs and Chinatown had grown up near the first mines, so I had a good view of everything. From Number Three mine I could see the Westerners gathering across the creek from Chinatown. Stars winked all along the line. Shading my eyes, I squinted and saw that it was the sunlight glinting off their gun barrels. It was funny that something deadly should look so pretty.

"The Chinese should leave Chinatown," I complained to Father, "before they're trapped."

Father's forehead wrinkled with worry. "That's what I told Ah Say. But he said I'm overreacting. He thinks the mob's just trying to scare the Chinese. He still insists the Company won't really let anything happen. He's sure that a mining official will show up and shoo the mob away."

I looked at all the guns sparkling down below. "I don't think any official is going to stop them this time."

Father tilted back his head like he always did when he was going to do something brave and foolish. "I'll go down again, and this time I'll make the Chinese leave town."

Father seemed determined to get himself killed, so I tried to stop that foolishness right away. "Ah Say's in charge, so if he says they should stay, they'll stay. I doubt if they'll listen to anyone else."

He glanced at me with a sad, crooked smile. "You mean especially if it's me."

I had always counted myself as being pretty smart; but suddenly I didn't know how to argue with him. All I could do was poke along—as if I were chipping away at a mountain with a dull pickax. "I'm sorry. I don't mean to hurt your feelings. But you could die down there. And for nothing."

Father turned away. "Well, at least I'd be consistent."

I felt like I was botching things badly; and yet if I failed, it would be the end of Father. "Why are you so bound on getting yourself shot?" I said frantically. "You can do more good if you stay alive."

"I have to make up for something," Father said.

"You mean because your uncle saved your life?" I asked.

"That and another man." Father hesitated and then went on. "I've never told anyone, but I killed a man back in China. A Manchu."

"Good, Fish Man," Bull grunted. "That's one less of that scum to get rid of when we take China back from them."

I just stared at Father. He was such a mild man that it was hard to believe. "How?"

"I was young and hot-blooded." He shrugged. "When you commit that kind of mistake, you try and make up for it the rest of your life."

Like fighting for so many good but hopeless causes. "I don't care," I blurted out. "You're my father, and I want you alive." As Father stared at me surprised, the words caught in my throat. "You're all I have."

The truth was so simple and easy; and yet it had taken me so long to realize it.

Bull was lying with the other four victims out in the sunshine. "Listen to your son, Fish Man. Stay out of Chinatown."

I waved a hand at the wagon we had borrowed to bring the injured to Number Three. "We have to get our friends back to Number Six. I can't manage it by myself."

Even now Father fretted over his responsibilities. "But what about the people in Chinatown?"

"What about your boy?" Bull demanded. "It'd be kinder to shoot him yourself than leave him an orphan in a foreign land."

Father looked guiltily at Chinatown and then back at

the bandage on my cheek that Dr. Langhorn had put there after tending to my other bruises. Finally he sighed. "Before he left, the doctor said Bull and the others should rest before we take them back to Six."

I had never expected to win, because I had never thought he would count me more important than his sense of duty. All I could do was stammer, "Th-thank you."

I could see his conscience was still pestering him. "I'm sorry, boy. I should have realized that I owe a debt to you, too," he said huskily, "more than to Uncle Foxfire or your cousins."

Bull stretched his arm up and gripped Father's hand. "There's a big difference between being a fool and being a coward."

Father squeezed Bull's fingers. "Thank you."

Bull closed his eyes. "But you're still an idiot, Fish Man."

CHAPTER | 42

Michael Purdy
Rock Springs
Wednesday, September 2
Afternoon

I ate as quick as I could and then headed out with a basket of laundry. Only I didn't deliver it. Folks were swarming from all over town like ants out of an old log, so I joined them and got a real earful.

Ma was wrong. The Patriots were done talking. Captain Jack and the committee had cooked up a scheme, and the Patriots had voted to serve it to the Chinese.

I joined the other folks aiming for the bridge where the Patriots were gathering. There were eighty miners or so, but I also saw Keenan, the gambler, as well some ex-railroad workers. All in all, I would have said there were another eighty mischief-makers from the town; and each and every one of them was armed with a gun, rifle, or shotgun. And by now there were as many watchers as there were warriors.

Across the bridge were the shacks of Chinatown. A huge

butte rose behind it, like a rocky wave that was going to crush it.

The Patriots themselves were buzzing with talk about the Chinese setting up barricades in Chinatown.

Dr. Murray was beside himself. "Why are we standing here? They're getting ready for a fight," he said to Captain Jack.

Captain Jack pulled a watch out of his pocket. "We gave them an hour to leave or else," he said.

"And look how they're using the time," Mrs. Reilly said. "I say we chase them out now."

"If you don't do something, I will." Mrs. Duval held up her pistol. "Who's with me?"

"I am," Johnson shouted, waving a gun in the air.

More of the Patriots began to take up the call. Captain Jack looked around, seeing the temper of the crowd. "All right. All right, we'll go."

Everyone began to hooraw again.

"You know what to do," the Captain said when the commotion had died down.

The Patriots split into two columns. Steve led the smaller one toward the plank bridge. Their boots thumped on the wooden boards, making it sound like a huge drum. On the other side of the creek Steve posted guards to watch the bridge. Then he fanned out the rest into a line and began to close slowly on Chinatown.

While Captain Jack led the second column along the near side of the creek, women and children began to climb on top of the boxcars for a better view. As I shinnied up one myself, I caught a lungful from inside. From the stink, it must have held cattle before and hadn't been cleaned out. Seth was on top with his bully boys.

I almost went back down, but the view was best from here. And Seth and his bully boys were too excited to notice me. They had bigger game today.

Squinting, I could make out Chinatown. I didn't see any barricades or armed Chinese. The few men in the streets were just ambling along like it was just another day. All I saw was the smoke of cooking fires rising lazily from the shacks. When the wind blew a certain way, I could smell frying meat. The only thing the Chinese were getting ready for was a meal.

Captain Jack marched the second column across the railroad bridge. They left a rear guard on one side of the bridge and then another guard on the other side, where Mrs. Reilly and some laundrywomen stayed.

Mrs. Duval, though, and the rest of the laundrywomen kept straight on with the main body—not toward Chinatown but toward mine Number Three.

Until then I'd reckoned the Patriots had been acting on the spur of the moment. But you don't move around like that without a plan. It was like a battle map in a history book, with the big arrows that stand for regiments of solders.

Except this wasn't war. This was cold-blooded murder. And maybe they'd head to mine Number Six next.

"Here they go." Seth swept his hat off and began to wave it. "Hooraw!"

CHAPTER | 43

Joseph Young
Mine Number Three
Wednesday, September 2
Afternoon

As the Westerners came up the hill shooting their guns in the air and hollering, I just stood there staring as if I were watching a play on a distant stage.

The shooting had panicked the mule, and the wagon had rattled off, so we were trapped. I looked around, but the miners at Number Three had vanished. One of them poked a head out of a doorway. "Don't stand out there," he called. "Get in here."

Father turned urgently to the stretchers. "Help me get these men inside."

Bull slapped Father's calf. "Fish Man, no door's going to keep them out. Take your boy and go."

Father licked his lips. "I'll go down and reason with the Westerners."

I saw a flash of light, and smoke puffed up with a little

popping noise. A moment later something whizzed by my ear and whacked into the dirt.

"They'll be too busy shooting to listen," Bull said, and swept up a pebble and threw it at me all in one motion. "Run, Fish Boy."

I flinched as it whizzed just above my head. "I can't leave you."

Bull waved at me to flee. "Will you listen to me for once? If you run, your father will follow."

It was the truth, but still I hesitated. "But you're our workmates," I protested.

"We're all dead men." He nodded to the buildings where the Number Three miners were. "And so are they." He threw another rock at me. "And so will you be if you stay with me."

This one hit me square in the chest. I bet he had been a real terror back in China chasing birds from the fields.

If I had been lying on the stretcher, I don't think I would have told my friends to abandon me. Bull had more courage than I would ever have.

"Bull's just being big winded again. Give me a hand," Father ordered.

But Bull was right. "We should go," I said.

The Westerners swirled around the lower building, where some of the Chinese had hidden. Someone began kicking at the door. The flimsy planks broke after a half dozen blows.

A Chinese burst through the doorway. There was a

bright flash of light and I heard the roar. And the Chinese went down.

Another Chinese fled down the slope away from the miners. I heard a shot and he fell forward, his body rolling and rolling.

"No, no," Father said, as if words could magically wash the scene all away. "This isn't supposed to happen. It doesn't make any sense."

"You won't do anyone any good dying with me," Bull said. Frustrated, he threw a rock so hard he winced at the pain the motion cost him. This one just narrowly missed, or I might have wound up on the ground with him.

"If I live, I'll do what I can for your family," I promised. Suddenly I wondered if this is what Father had done for Uncle Foxfire.

Bull nodded to me and then turned slightly to aim a rock at Father. "Go after your boy."

I had already started to run. Behind me the Western miners whooped and hollered. There were lots of gunshots now and men beginning to scream.

I twisted my head around. In the distance Bull was throwing rocks as bullets zipped around him; Father was running after me.

"They'll go to the other camps. We've got to head into the wastelands," he called.

"Without food or water?" I asked. "And we don't have blankets. It was freezing inside the cabin this morning.

Imagine what it will be like outside at night."

"And there are wolves too," Father said. "But it's suicide to enter the town."

"So that's the last place they think we'll go." Something stuck in mind from Miss Virginia's vocabulary lessons, and suddenly the word *sanctuary* rang clear and loud as a church bell inside my mind. She had said if fugitives could reach a church and claim sanctuary, they would be safe.

And I knew where we needed to go. Someplace where even the miners couldn't harm us.

"We'll claim *sanctuary*," I said. We had no other choice.

CHAPTER | 44

Michael Purdy
Rock Springs
Wednesday, September 2
Afternoon

Seth was leaning so far forward, he almost fell off the boxcar. "I wish I had a telescope," he said.

Number Three was too far away to see much. At this distance I couldn't tell the Patriots from the Chinese as they scurried around like ants. I heard the faint *pop–pop–pop*—like firecrackers. Smoke rose in quick puffs like a field of fluffy white flowers.

It would have been almost pretty, except some of the ants fell down and stopped moving. And the Patriots kept right on going through the mine shooting and killing.

I stood there in shock. The Patriots were neighbors. Even if they hadn't been friendly to me, I'd seen them be loving toward their families. They couldn't be killers.

Then the Patriots at the mine flowed back down the hill, fanning out into a line to join with Steve's bunch sweeping in from the plank bridge. It was like a noose closing around the throat of Chinatown.

They paused at the edge. I hoped it was their consciences finally catching up with them. Suddenly I heard the crack of a gunshot like a board breaking. It made me jump. Then I started to hear shots, ragged at first, like ice breaking on a pond.

Grimly the Patriots began to close in. There were more single gunshots. After a few of those, all of them began raising their guns. Even then I didn't think they'd go through with it.

The next moment all the rifles spat little tongues of flame—as if Chinatown were wearing a necklace of tiny fiery needles. Smoke started to billow over their heads, and I heard the thunder of the massed guns.

Suddenly a cabin door flew open, and a Chinese scampered out into the street. In his hand he held a handkerchief stuffed with whatever he had tried to save. Another door banged open, and out burst more Chinese. They were barefoot, but they had their belongings rolled up in blankets. I could see them trying to escape all through Chinatown.

Doors opened all over, as if the houses and shacks were getting ready to scream. Chinese flowed out of in streams of solid blue because of their shirts and coats. But there was nowhere to run. The Patriots surrounded them.

When the Patriots fired once again, I told myself they were shooting overhead to scare off the Chinese. So when I saw the Chinese start to crumple to the dirt, I didn't believe it at first. I didn't want to.

And the Patriots kept on shooting volley after volley. On and on.

Chinese fell everywhere. The ground was covered with them. They looked like little dolls that a child had dropped on the street—almost like they were playing a game with the Patriots and just pretending. Except around each blue doll was a red circle that slowly widened.

"Stop it, stop it!" I heard someone shouting. When the shooting died down, I realized it was me.

For a moment the Patriots stood frozen in place, as if I were staring at a picture. Only the rising gun smoke told me otherwise. It drifted upward in dozens of threads that mixed overhead into a large cloud.

Faintly I heard one of the wounded Chinese begin calling something in a ragged, hurt voice. I was sure he was asking for help.

When he reckoned it was safe, the doctor spurred his white horse to the very front, waving his hat. "At 'em, boys. Shoot them down. For your families! For your homes! No quarter!"

"No quarter!" a dozen voices roared in agreement. A ragged cheer went up from the watchers; but there weren't nearly as many hoorawing now.

As the Patriots started forward, they broke into squads of eight to ten men—but I saw some women, too, like Mrs.

Duval. They began breaking into the cabins and shacks.

The Chinese who had tried to hide in Chinatown broke from cover now. The Patriots swept them up neatly. Some of the Patriots had each Chinese hand over his valuables and then let him go. Of course, that was no guarantee the next squad was going to free him.

Other Chinese were clubbed with pistols and rifle butts. Then their limp bodies were cleaned out of anything they had.

The more "sporting" made a game of it, chasing down the running Chinese as if the Patriots were hounds and the Chinese antelopes. Then the Patriots would throw them to the ground. After beating and robbing them, they let them go.

But some squads still had the blood lust, killing any Chinese they saw.

I was shocked when I saw Mrs. Duval shoot one Chinese and get another with two more shots.

The Patriots who didn't do any shooting or clubbing stood around and cheered and clapped for the ones who did.

A few Chinese managed to break through. Some of them hightailed it for the railroad bridge. One suddenly clutched his head and fell backward. When I looked at the guards, I realized with a shock that it was Mrs. Reilly who had aimed the pistol. Another laundrywoman shot two more Chinese in the chest, and a third fell on the riverbank.

"Stop shooting!" I called to them. "It's over. They're leaving."

"Not fast enough." Seth grinned. "At 'em, boys." Snatching the hat from his head, he began waving it and whooping.

The doctor was riding back and forth through the streets of Chinatown, still waving his own hat. Faintly I heard him shouting, "No quarter." Suddenly he twisted in his saddle and waved his hand at two running Chinese. "Shoot them down."

Some of the squads must have still been seaching in Chinatown, because I could still hear them at work. Gunshots and screams, gunshots and screams. And I could do nothing to stop it. I wanted to cover up my ears, but then I would have felt like a coward.

That fool Seth picked up on the doctor's battle cry. "No quarter!"

I gave him a shove. "This isn't war. This is a slaughter!"

He skidded a step on top of the boxcar and whirled around angrily. "They asked for it."

Suddenly I saw more Chinese flood from behind the town toward the hills to the southeast and Burning Mountain. They must have found a hole in the line.

Seth threw back his head. "Hoo-ee, look at 'em run. Just like scared jackrabbits."

Fred looked a little sick. So did some of the other bully boys; but Fred forced himself to grin weakly. "From the way they're bounding, they're more like antelopes."

Seth folded his arms. "'Minds me of sheep. They won't stop running till they reach San Francisco."

I started praying Joseph would be one of those who would be able to get away if they went to Number Six. When I saw the squads appear on the other side of the town, I reckoned they would turn around and come back; but they kept right on marching, following the Chinese. Every now and then they'd pause long enough to take a shot. The distance reduced the shots to popping noises.

The Patriots didn't stop until they ran out of targets. Then they swung back. In the meantime the doctor had put some Patriots to setting up a bonfire out of wood. I could see him gesturing to brands.

As the Patriots passed by, they snatched up burning boards and sticks and headed into Chinatown. They weren't going to leave one shack standing.

I was surprised to see there were still Chinese hiding in Chinatown. The last survivors burst from the burning buildings. Around their heads they had clothing or blankets against the flames. It didn't protect them against the bullets, though.

And then the screams began from inside the flaming shacks. There must have been some who had tried to ride it out inside their homes.

One Chinese was hiding in an outhouse. The Patriots dragged him kicking and shouting and threw him into a burning shack.

I'd just about had my fill of the Patriots, of people, of everything.

"You've got what you want," I shouted at them. "Stop, for Heaven's sake!"

"They'll think twice before they show their pigtails here again," Fred said smugly.

"You know," Seth said to the bully boys, "it was payday a couple of days ago. There'll be rich pickings, boys."

Fred glanced at Chinatown. "You mean go into there?"

Seth slapped him on the back. "Not yet. We'll let the Patriots finish cleaning the rats out of Chinatown first."

I couldn't take it any longer. "What's wrong with you? They're people, not animals."

Fred and some of the other bully boys looked like they agreed; but Seth spun around. "Why are you sticking up for those varmints? Little Chinese lover." Seth swore, and before I could duck, he swung his arm in a backhanded slap that knocked me off the boxcar.

CHAPTER | 45

Joseph Young
Rock Springs
Wednesday, September 2
Late afternoon

We had circled around, keeping low, as the miners who had attacked Number Three turned and joined the others surrounding Chinatown. It was just as I thought: Rock Springs was the last place they expected a Chinese would head. They had their backs to us.

However, when we reached the creek, we were stuck at first; but then I noticed animal tracks leading into the water. "This must be a ford," I said.

We splashed across. There were dozens of little huts dug into the sides of the creek bank, but no one seemed to be home. Cautiously we climbed the bank, moving between deserted shacks until we crossed the railroad track before it split into many separate lines. As we snuck through the town, I heard a hiss. I was so tense that I must have jumped a couple of feet in the air. When I turned, I saw two fellow classmates, Paul and Thomas, come out from an alley where they must have been hiding.

Even though Paul wore a Chinese shirt and pants, he also wore a derby hat like a badge. Thomas had pulled on a brown American coat.

"I saw them on my way in. They're killing everyone in Chinatown," Paul said, panting.

Father glanced at the ugly cloud of smoke writhing into the sky. "And burning everything too."

"Are you also going to the church for sanctuary?" Thomas asked, shivering.

"We've gotten around the mob. Maybe we should get to our camp," Father said.

"What's going to keep the mob from going there next?" I asked.

Father looked as if he were going to argue, but then the wind whipped a swirl of black smoke down around us and he began to cough. Suddenly he sagged. "Have I been wrong all the time about things? All that talk about peace and getting along—maybe those have just been pretty paper butterflies too."

I never thought I'd hear him admit that. And I didn't want him to now. "No, you were right, Father." I thought about Star Rock. It was everything Father could have wished. "You and Uncle Sean. Michael and me. It isn't a dream."

Father stared at me. "But you said I was a fool."

"No," I said. "I was the fool. You have the right dream. There just to have be more of us making that dream happen."

Father looked at me and then sighed. "When did you grow up?"

I grinned. "Right now the main thing is to survive."

The few people on the street were silent at first, but the deeper we went into town, the more people began to jeer—though as yet no one had made a move to stop us.

"This is a mistake," Father said, glancing around, worried.

It was strange. I had walked through this area so many times before that I took it for granted. Now I began to imagine hordes of killers hiding behind every door. So I was glad when I saw the church steeple. "Come on," I said to Father, and broke into a trot, as did the others.

We raced past the Westerners straight for the church. As I went up the steps, I began to shout, *"Sanctuary."*

Paul beat me to the door and tugged at the big brass handle; but the door wouldn't open. He tugged at it frantically and then gave up, banging on the planks, begging for help in Chinese and frantically repeating, *"Hello, hello, hello."*

Father reached around him to haul at it too. "It's locked."

"The rectory," Thomas said, but Paul was already darting

toward the house next door. He seized the brass door knocker and began banging at it, while the others began pounding at the wooden panels with their fists.

"*Miss Virginia, help,*" Thomas called.

The door stayed closed. But a little window opened at eye level. "Yes?" The voice was Miss Virginia's.

The relief washed over me like a wave. "We're safe," I said to Father, and then repeated our lesson faithfully to our English teacher. "*We want to claim sanctuary. They're killing all the Chinese.*"

I saw her eye dart toward me, and one eyebrow rose in recognition. "*Just a minute.*"

The little window closed, and I began to relax as we waited for her to open the door. However, when the seconds became minutes and the door remained shut, I began to feel uncomfortable. It didn't help any that hostile townsfolk had begun to gather around us in a circle.

I was so sure that someone was going to rush from some unseen angle that I kept turning round and round like a top.

Paul and Thomas began to pound on the door again. "*Miss Virginia, help. Please let us in.*"

They nearly fell in when the door jerked open. We started to surge forward, but she held us back with her arm.

"*I'm sorry. You can't stay here,*" she said. Her eyes twitched nervously around at the crowd.

I said the magical word again. *"Sanctuary."*

Miss Virginia raised a hand to her mouth as she remembered the vocabulary word she had taught us. *"That only works for Christians, which you're not. And anyway, that riffraff don't respect traditions. You won't be safe here. You're better off leaving town."*

Before I could explain, Thomas began bowing and pleading, *"Help us."*

"Virginia, let them in!" Miss Evangeline said from behind her.

Miss Virginia was staring at the Westerners gathering behind us. *"I'm sorry. It's for the best if you go."* She looked in tears as she slowly began to close the door.

"You can't leave them out there," Miss Evangeline said.

Her protests faded away as the door shut.

Paul was pounding on the door. *"Sanctuary, sanctuary,"* he kept saying over and over. I'd taught him the word. But there was only silence from the door now.

"How could she?" I asked. She was my teacher. Hadn't I done everything she asked? My mind felt numb, as if someone had exploded a keg of powder inside me. Was this how Father had felt when he'd seen all his own dreams blasted away?

And when I turned, I saw the crowd had started to grin and close in.

"What's the matter, monkeys?" jeered a fat slug of a man.

"Come on," Father said, and took my arm. "Walk slow.

Don't show you're afraid." Pivoting, he began to walk toward the crowd.

As the crowd edged in toward us, someone said, *"Monkeys, monkeys."*

And the others took up the chant as they began punching and kicking us. I lost my hat and Father lost his coat, but somehow we made it through standing up. Paul and Thomas were screaming from the rectory.

"We can't help them," Father said, blocking a punch with his forearm. "We've got to go."

"Where?" I asked as I ducked a fist.

"Anywhere but here." We took to our heels. I heard the Westerners laughing as they chased us. However, either we were in better shape than them or our fear was greater than their anger; we soon left them behind.

As we leaned against a house, trying to catch our breath, Father panted, "We'll have . . . to try . . . our luck . . . in the wastelands."

"There's my friend, Michael," I suggested.

While Father had been running, his queue had flopped over his chest. He draped it down his back again. "Why would . . . he take us . . . when the church lady . . . wouldn't?"

That was true enough. When it came to solutions, I was as much of a dinosaur as Bull. I bit my lip. "I can't say why. . . . Except he's . . . my friend."

Father studied me for a moment. "Out of all . . . the

people . . . in the camps . . . you could . . . find only. . . an outsider . . . to talk to?"

I shrugged uncomfortably. "He's . . . like me."

He leaned forward, resting his hands on his knees as he stared at the ground. "I should . . . have taken you . . . back to China."

"This is . . . my home," I insisted.

He glanced at me sadly. "A home . . . that doesn't . . . want us."

"Let's just . . . try to live . . . through today," I said.

While we got our breath back, I tried to remember everything Michael had told me about his house. I couldn't recall the number, but I remembered the street.

When we were ready, we started on again, hurrying through streets and alleys as I hunted for Michael's house. I nearly missed it, because the pencil drawings had almost faded to the color of the gray, unpainted boards. But I could make out the faint outlines of flowers behind a fence.

"The ghost garden," I murmured, remembering Michael's odd description.

"Considering . . . how close . . . we are . . . to becoming . . . ghosts, I guess . . . it's fitting," he puffed.

"This has to be Michael's house," I said. There could only be one building like that in Rock Springs.

As we hurried around the side, the flowers continued along the boards. Father stared at them. "Why . . . is it . . . like this?"

"Michael said they never got around to painting over it," I said as I peeked through a window. To my disappointment, though, there was no sign of my friend.

Leaving Father to get his breath back, I crawled along the wall. I could hear the echoes of shots and screams in the distance as I crept along and looked in the other windows. I didn't see Michael though—only a tired-looking woman in the kitchen. She had to be his mother.

We'd have to wait. As I crept back to Father, I hoped my friend was all right. Michael was almost as unpopular with the townsfolk as we were.

Father sat slumped against the wall, still panting.

I had noticed a rain barrel at the side of the house. "Do you want some water?"

When he nodded his head, I started back to the rain barrel. But as I slid back the heavy lid, the back door opened.

"*Michael, Michael Purdy. Is that you?*" a woman called. I started to get up to run when the woman stepped round the corner. The moment she saw us, she raised her apron to her lips. "*Lord preserve us.*"

"*Michael is my friend,*" I said. I pointed to Father. "*And that's my father.*"

She lowered the apron. "*Michael wouldn't be friends with any Chinese.*"

"*Yes, he is. Please help us,*" I begged.

She glanced around nervously, because it was risky to

be seen talking with us. *"You don't know what you're asking. It's too dangerous,"* she said, shaking her head.

Father touched my shoulder. "She's going to be like that woman at the church. We'd better find another place to hide."

As we started to turn away, Mrs. Purdy said, *"Wait."* She stepped closer. *"You're cut, boy."*

"It's okay," I said, trying to smile, but it hurt too much.

She clicked her tongue. *"And those bruises."* She twisted her apron tighter and tighter in her hands until it was a rope. Suddenly she beckoned. *"You'd better come inside for a while."*

I stood there stupidly, hardly believing my ears. She gestured impatiently for us to follow. *"I said come inside. I know how I'd feel if a mob was after Michael."*

We'd found our sanctuary at last.

CHAPTER | 46

Michael Purdy
Chinatown
Wednesday, September 2
Late afternoon

I woke when the smoke started to tickle my nose. And when I tried to take a deep breath, I only got more smoke. I sat up coughing. At first I thought Seth and his bully boys had thrown me on top of a bonfire, and I punched around me frantically. But then I realized it wasn't hot enough.

Opening my eyes, I saw the sun hanging behind a curtain of smoke. It glowed a blood red, like an open wound in the sky. The air smelled funny too, but I couldn't quite place it.

All around me folks were hoorawing like we'd won the biggest battle ever, and I could see that Seth and his bully boys had climbed down from the boxcar top.

As he swung back toward town, one of the bully boys complained, "I thought we were going to see what we could find in Chinatown?"

"That can wait," Seth said excitedly. "I've been waiting all my life to see someone pay back all the skunks in town."

From the bridge came the thumping of many feet. I reckoned the noble Patriots were on the march again, spoiling for a fight with more defenseless folk. My back ached, and I felt a little groggy as I got to my feet.

All the other watchers were hurrying over to line the path and cheer on their brave protectors.

The doctor led them all on his white horse. He raised his hat, nodding to one side and then to the other. Captain Jack stomped along beside him, waving a hand as well.

Mrs. Reilly, Mrs. Duval, and the other laundrywomen were sashaying just behind them in the place of honor. And then the Patriots swaggered along, with their rifles draped over their shoulders, or their hands on their belts near their revolvers. Seth and the bully boys were walking along with long strides, trying to keep up with the Patriots.

I couldn't see the bodies in Chinatown anymore because of the big cloud of black smoke rising from there now. At its base fiery demons danced and played. There wasn't much chance of anybody being alive in that.

All around Chinatown was a ring of blue. If you didn't look close, the bodies looked like a meadow of blue wildflowers had suddenly bloomed around the fire. They dotted the ground up to the creek and all the way up the slopes.

I heard groans and calls in Chinese—I figured for help—so not all of them were dead; but I didn't know how they would do when it was night. It got downright chilly once the sun set.

I would have reckoned the Patriots had had their fill of killing by now, but only half of them returned to town. I saw other groups marching off. I guess toward the other mines. Maybe they were heading to Number Six.

I should have gone on to warn Joseph. If I ran, I might get ahead of the Patriots. But then the miners might do to me what they'd done to the Chinese. So, feeling like a monstrous coward and traitor, I turned my back on my only friend. I just hoped Joseph and his pa got away somehow; but I'd see to my own hide first.

As I slunk along all hangdog, the Cranleys passed by me, walking quickly. Emily, their little girl, was looking as sick as I felt. "Couldn't they have just chased the Chinese away?" she asked in a high, piping voice.

"What would have kept them from coming back?" Mr. Cranley argued. "They had plenty of warning to go."

I wanted to tell them about Joseph, but I held my tongue like the coward I was and I just joined the spectators going home.

When we reached the edge of town, Emily took her ma's hand. "I want to go home."

"If you want," Mrs. Cranley said. She looked glad of an excuse.

Mr. Cranley ran a hand over his bald head. "I know it was pretty harsh; but what choice did they leave us? We had to teach them a lesson."

"Not this way," Mrs. Cranley snapped, and headed away. While some of the watchers followed the parade like Mr. Cranley, most of them peeled away like his wife and daughter. I think they'd had enough of the Patriots' schooling.

I was sick of it too; and yet it was also like being on a runaway wagon. I wound up tagging along with Mr. Cranley. And as we walked down the streets, I saw shades and curtains drawn on a lot of windows like the folks inside were hiding themselves. Every now and then, I thought I saw a curtain part and an eye peek out. But the curtain closed up just as fast. Not everybody was proud of what was happening.

"This way, this way," Mrs. Reilly said, waving her hand to a side street.

Captain Jack, though, pointed in another direction. "But Kincaid's is over here."

Mrs. Duval tossed her head at the captain as she passed him. "We helped you. Now it's your turn to help us laundrywomen get rid of the Chinese taking our customers."

"We have to keep to our objectives," Captain Jack insisted.

Johnson pushed past Captain Jack to join Mrs. Reilly. "She makes a better captain than you do," he said.

As the Patriots swung around slowly to follow Mrs. Reilly, the captain tried to save his reputation. "This way, boys," he said, as if it was his idea.

Mrs. Reilly and Mrs. Duval led us straight to Ah Lee's laundry.

Mrs. Duval brandished her pistol. "Come on out, you skunk."

However, the laundry door remained shut.

"Don't you know to answer a lady?" Seth took a couple of running steps and then threw a rock, which crashed through the window. In the wink of an eye his bully boys were copying him, and the window was soon in a hundred pieces.

As a few last bits of glass fell from the window frame, Captain Jack jumped through the window. "This way, boys."

Holding up his gun, Jake jumped over the sill after the captain. Their boots crunched the broken glass as they disappeared into the shadows, but we could hear them calling inside, "Where are you, you varmint?"

Mrs. Reilly stood by the broken window. "Captain, what's taking you so long?" she called inside.

"Can't find anyone," Captain Jack hollered back.

"Wait. I got a locked door," Jake yelled.

There was a lot of hollering for Ah Lee to come out; but of course he didn't—any more than I would have.

So Captain Jack led his Patriots back out of the laundry and sent them up to the roof and had them go over to the spot above where they judged Ah Lee was hiding. With their rifle butts, they tried to break through the roof; but it was thicker than they'd reckoned, so the captain got impatient. "This is taking too long. Give him some warning shots."

Jake reversed his gun and pumped a couple of shots

below. The next moment the Patriots were diving as Ah Lee answered back with bullets of his own.

Captain Jack crawled to the edge of the roof so he could shout down angrily at the street. "Why didn't you warn us that he was armed?"

"Men!" Mrs. Reilly snorted. "If you won't get him, I will."

Steve stopped her. "Allow me," he said, plunging in.

A couple of other Patriots charged after him. I heard the crash of boards and then more shots. It sounded like there was a fight inside.

"Here's the skunk," Steve shouted in triumph. He came to the window leading Ah Lee by his queue. Ah Lee tried to lean toward him to ease the pain. "Please, please, I leave."

"Then git." He kicked Ah Lee in the pants.

That drew such a laugh from the Patriots and the spectators that Steve grinned, pleased. "Greedy pig, we warned you." And he repeated the punishment. This time there was applause.

Ah Lee waved his hands in the air frantically. "I go, I go." From his coat pocket came a little bag of penny candy. It fell in the street, where sugary sweets went rolling through the dirt.

Mrs. Duval was waiting by the broken window. "Steal the bread from my children's mouths, will you?" She spat at Ah Lee.

"You apologize to the lady," Steve said; and with a sudden yank, he sent Ah Lee forward through the window frame and out in the street.

"Sorry, sorry," Ah Lee wailed from the dirt. "I leave. I not come back. Never."

"You bet you won't." Mr. Keenan in his silk vest strode forward. Before anyone realized what he was going to do, Mr. Keenan had cocked his gun and shot Ah Lee through the head.

I shut my eyes, but not fast enough; and I knew the sight was going to stay with me for the rest of my life.

As Ah Lee thumped backward, Mrs. Duval looked a little surprised. Then she looked down at her skirt and wiped absentmindedly at the spots of blood.

Suddenly a woman I didn't know ran forward. I could see the tears streaking the dirt and smoke on her cheeks. "This is for my baby," she said, and jumped on top of the corpse, her heels landing with a thump. Shaking with rage, she began an odd little dance upon her human stage. "And this is for his pain. If it hadn't been for your kind, I could have bought medicine."

Nobody knew what to make of it. Mrs. Reilly tried to reach a hand out to her. "All right, Mabel."

"She's gone cuckoo," Seth muttered to one of the bully boys.

Everyone else just watched for a moment, as if this was too savage even for them. Then Captain Jack announced in a shaky voice, "Back to our objectives, men."

I think the Patriots were glad for a reason to leave. "On

to Kincaid's," Steve yelled. He was going to keep that promise he'd made.

"Yes, on to Kincaid's." Still waving his pistol over his head, Captain Jack strode down the street, and the rest of the crowd fell into step behind him. By now spectators and Patriots were intermingled. The doctor and his horse were somewhere in the middle. As Mabel continued to dance upon Ah Lee's corpse, the passel of them took to their heels, except for Mrs. Duval and Mrs. Reilly and me.

"Mabel," Mrs. Reilly said gently.

Panting, Mabel stopped. She was still trembling. "He owes me."

"I know he does." Mrs. Duval took the woman's elbow.

"I'm not finished yet," Mabel protested, but she let Mrs. Duval haul her down off the corpse.

"Of course not," Mrs. Duval said soothingly, and set her own pistol down on the dirt.

I thought she was going to lead Mabel away, but instead Mrs. Duval hoisted up her skirts and stepped through the broken window. "And anyone who patronized this dog owes you too."

Mrs. Duval had still kept hold of Mabel, so Mabel had no choice but to climb through the window after her. She shuffled in a daze as Mrs. Duval led her behind the counter.

Mrs. Reilly fidgeted like a hound dog that's caught the scent as the tail end of the Patriots left. "Let's go," she called.

"You go without us," Mrs. Duval said. "We've got something to do."

"Catch up with me later," Mrs. Reilly said, and almost skipped after the others.

I watched in amazement as Mrs. Duval calmly studied the labels on the blue packages. Finally she just gave up. "I can't make head nor tail of these hen scratchings."

Taking one blue-papered parcel from the shelf, she began tearing at it. "Oh, now these shirts would look good on your husband."

"This is like Christmas." Mabel brightened. She turned to the shelves and began ripping open the packages just where they sat.

The smoke from Chinatown was still tickling my nose. Suddenly I realized what the funny scent was.

Mixed with the smell of burning wood was the odor of cooking meat.

I'd seen and heard enough to make me sick of the whole human race.

CHAPTER | 47

Mrs. Purdy shoved us into the house and then ran around closing the curtains, muttering over and over, *"What's a body to do?"*

"I wish Michael had been here," I whispered to Father. "He could have smoothed things over. She really doesn't want us."

"Can you blame her? If the mob finds out she's helped us, they'll kill her and your friend too," Father said.

Mrs. Purdy rushed into the next room to cover the windows. I tried to distract myself by studying the room. It was even more barren than our camp cabin: There was only a cot. The rest of the furniture was just penciled outlines on the walls.

"Your friend was right. It's a ghost house," Father said, and waved his hand toward the outside. "Just like

235

it's a ghost garden out there."

I jumped when I heard gunshots. "They sound closer."

Mrs. Purdy came rushing back in. *"I think the mob's coming back into town."*

Father glanced at me and then said, *"We'll go. We can't bring trouble down on your head."*

"If I had my druthers, I wouldn't have you under my roof even in peaceful times." It was blunt, yet I would rather have her be honest than a hypocrite like Miss Virginia. *"But I wouldn't turn a dog over to that mob, let alone a boy. So get into the cellar."* And she jerked open a door.

We stumbled down the steps in the darkness. When she lit a kerosene lantern a moment later, I saw that the cellar was filled with tubs and laundry lines.

"You should be safe here for now," she said. She glanced up the stairs. *"But where is that boy?"*

"Don't you know where Michael is?" I asked.

"No," she said, shaking her head. *"I wish I did."*

Suddenly I started to worry.

CHAPTER | 48

Michael Purdy
Rock Springs
Wednesday, September 2
Late afternoon

Ma pounced on me as soon as I got back. "Where have you been? Don't you realize you scared me half to death?" she demanded, but then she saw my face. "What's wrong, Michael?" She pushed the hair from my eyes.

"I saw . . . I saw . . ." The words choked in my throat for a moment. "They killed Chinese like they were animals. And they threw them alive into burning buildings. They even shot Ah Lee and then danced on his body."

She hugged me to her. I couldn't remember when she had done that last. "You're too young to see so much ugliness," she whispered.

For a moment I was too stunned to think anything except how strong she was. All that washing had made her forearms strong as a miner's.

I guess a body can get attached even to a low-down dog like me, or maybe it was just habit with Ma. "I'm sorry I worried you," I said.

Her hand felt the lump on my head. "What happened?"

"Seth knocked me off a boxcar," I said, squirming.

"What were you doing on top—?" She started to hold me at arm's length but saw my face. "Well, you tell me when you're ready."

I breathed a sigh of relief. "Thank you."

"But this can't wait. Do you know what the Patriots might be doing now?" she asked.

I remembered some of what I had overheard. "Some of them have gone on to the other camps to get the Chinese there. The ones in town are hunting down the Chinese or the Chinese lovers."

Ma bit her lip. "I was afraid of that."

"What's wrong?" I asked, puzzled.

Ma took several long, calming breaths. "We . . . we have guests." Turning, she went to the cellar and opened the door. The kerosene lantern was already lit below so we had no trouble going down the stairs.

"Michael?" a familiar voice asked.

I nearly fell down the rest of the way when I saw my friend getting to his feet. His father still crouched by a laundry tub.

"Joseph?" I went down the rest of the steps, afraid that I was dreaming, afraid that he was a ghost like me. And then I turned to Ma.

"You hid them?" I asked. I knew how she hated Chinese.

Ma shrugged uncomfortably. "I couldn't leave them to likes of that mob."

I wrapped my arms around and held her tight. Even if I was a low-down crawfish, Ma could stand up to a whole town, guns and all.

CHAPTER | 49

Joseph Young
Rock Springs
Wednesday, September 2
Late afternoon

I was real glad to see Michael again. *"We were worried about you,"* I said.

Michael just stared at me. *"You're alive."*

"Thanks to your mother." I motioned to Father. *"I think you remember my father."*

Embarrassed, Father rose and extended his hand. The last time they had met, the camp had been running him off. *"Hello. I'm sorry for that other day."*

Michael took his and shook it. *"After what I've seen today, I don't blame you for not trusting Americans. Anyway, that all seems kind of small now. They're killing Chinese wherever they find them."*

"It's too dangerous for you then. We'll go," Father insisted.

Mrs. Purdy shook her head. *"Don't worry about us. We'll manage. We always have. You'll leave only when it's safe to do so. I'll have no part of this madness."*

They argued for a while, but for once Father had met someone even more stubborn than him. Mrs. Purdy folded her arms. *"Do you want more food?"*

Father pointed to the plate of sandwiches and tea she had already brought down for us. *"We're fine."*

Mrs. Purdy nodded. *"I'll bring down spare blankets. It looks like you may be here for a while. Is there anything else you'll need?"*

Father glanced toward the parlor and then asked, *"Have you got some colored paper?"*

Mrs. Purdy looked puzzled. *"Whatever for?"*

"Miss Evie gave me some," Michael offered.

"Wouldn't you rather have plain, if you want to write letters?" Mrs. Purdy asked, puzzled.

"And maybe scissors?" Father asked.

"There're a couple of pair over there," Mrs. Purdy pointed to her sewing table.

"They will do just fine," Father said.

"But can you see well enough for what you want to do?" Mrs. Purdy nodded to the kerosene lamp casting a dim light.

"I'm used to working by moonlight," Father said. He'd often made his cutouts at night outside the cabin.

I couldn't see why he had to do that at a time like this. I guess old habits die hard.

CHAPTER | 50

Michael Purdy
Rock Springs
Wednesday, September 2
Dusk

If I were hiding from murderers, I reckon I wouldn't be fretting about paper and scissors. I fetched them anyway for the Youngs. Joseph seemed embarrassed, but his father looked happy enough when I handed them over.

When I started to wash up in the kitchen, I noticed the smoke had drifted into this part of town now. It made my stomach queasy, but my conscience felt even queasier. So far Ma had done more for my friends than I had.

Ma folded her arms as she watched me. "That boy, Joseph, says he's your friend. That right?"

I had been afraid of this moment. "Yes'm."

"How did you meet him?" Ma asked.

I thought about lying; but Ma was watching me real steady, and I lost the gumption. So I tried telling her the truth for a change. "We found all sorts of fossils at this place we call Star Rock. And bones, lots and lots of them."

Ma looked puzzled for a moment. "Bones?"

"Like Pa used to hunt," I said. "

I waited for Ma to explode, but instead she let her breath out slowly like her chest hurt her. "Ah."

I hadn't meant to, but I'd done it again to Ma. "I'm sorry, Ma. I won't ever mention him again."

"But a Chinese boy? Land, why make friends with the likes of them?" she wondered out loud.

Ma knew I was a traitor now. "Well, he was there already. He found it first."

She set her hands on my shoulders, so I had to look her square in the face. "Couldn't you have gone there with American friends instead?"

How could I tell her about being the ghost boy? "They aren't interested in old bones," I fibbed a little, "like Joseph."

She got real suspicious. "A dog doesn't get chummy with a skunk if it's got a choice. If you had any other friends, you never would have needed a Chinese one."

"You're wrong, Ma. I got lots of friends," I mumbled. "I'm sorry. I know you think I'm a low-down snake for making friends with a Chinese."

As Ma stared at me, I thought I'd done it now: She must really hate me.

But then I saw the tears at the corners of her eyes. "You must have been so lonesome, Mike. I'm sorry." She wiped her the back of her hand across her face. "It's just that . . . well,

I loved your pa so much; and when I lost him, I nearly went crazy inside. So I closed my eyes to everything, including you."

That caught me by surprise. "You mean you weren't mad at me?"

Ma put a hand on my cheek. The strong soaps had made her palm tough as leather, but I wouldn't have traded it for all the velvet in the world. "For what?"

"For being born," I mumbled.

I reckon I'd stretched the truth so many times that the poor thing just snapped. "Oh, Mike. What have I done to you?"

I didn't know what to think anymore. "If it wasn't for me, you could have left and started over again."

Ma shook her head. "We didn't leave because we didn't have the money. And"—she looked around at the ghostly furniture—"I guess I didn't want to leave the house your pa bought for us."

"So that's why we stayed," I said. We got stuck just like the shells and dinosaurs in the rocks.

She hugged me for the second time that day. "I'm just so sorry."

"Don't feel bad, Ma," I told her. "I've made enough bother for you already."

"Land, you're no bother," she said, squeezing harder.

I didn't believe her for a minute, but I liked the fact that she tried to lie. I don't think I would have cried if Ma had been her usual self. But the softness just made me bawl like a baby.

And all the awful things I'd seen just came out of me. "How could they? They're our neighbors. I always thought they were just folks like us. But they're monsters."

Ma rocked me back and forth. "They're not really monsters. They've got reasons to be mad, and they're afraid. Being afraid can make you do crazy things. I'm still mad at the Chinese myself."

"But you wouldn't kill them," I pointed out.

"No," Ma allowed, "because no matter what the reason, it's wrong to kill."

"Then why are they doing those terrible things?" I asked, bewildered.

"They're scared too," Ma explained. "So they don't see that the Chinese are folks just like them. The Chinese are just the enemy."

"But they're going after Mr. Kincaid as well," I said.

"He sides with the Chinese," Ma explained. "So that makes him an enemy too."

"All these respectable folk are so smug. But they're worse than us," I said. "We'd never hurt anyone just because we were afraid of them."

"I hope not, sugar," she said, patting me on the back. Then she let me go. "We can't judge them, Mike. A lot of bad things start out with good people trying to do something for the right reasons."

Something caught in my throat. "Like me? Your life would have been a lot better if I hadn't ruined it."

"That was love, plain and simple, Mike," Ma said. "I may not have shown it, but I would have hanged myself if it hadn't been for you. I'm going to make it up to you from now on. Starting with some food."

Ma put out a plate of sandwiches. I didn't have much appetite, but Ma hounded me until I took a bite. And at the first taste of food, I couldn't stop.

I had to admit I felt better the more my belly filled up. And then I remembered the basket I had left. "I got to pick up the laundry."

"Forget that," Ma said.

I would have been glad of the excuse, but I kept thinking over how big a coward I'd been earlier. It had been Ma and not me who had saved my friend.

"But," I said, "shouldn't we know what the Patriots are up to?"

Ma glanced nervously toward the street and then back at me. "Sure, but it's not safe."

"I'll keep out of sight," I said. "I got a lot of practice at it."

"Haven't you seen enough for one day?" Ma asked.

"Yeah," I admitted, but I nodded toward the cellar. "But it's not just me anymore. There are my friends. And then there's you."

Ma looked at me and then gave me a little push away. "You're growing up. Just don't do anything foolish."

It took all my nerve to step outside; and I used every trick I'd learned as a ghost boy to sneak through the town. Normally it would have taken only ten minutes to fetch the basket, but I floated through the town, hiding whenever I heard anyone.

All the stores and houses were shut up tight. Mr. Kincaid's was. So was Mr. Spenser's. I wondered if the Patriots had done to them what they had done to Ah Lee.

I didn't see the Patriots though. There were only folks coming back from the direction of Chinatown. As I hid in an alley, I saw that some of the townsfolk were guiding flocks of stolen chickens or ducks or geese. Others were leading pigs. One woman had a silk coat. Still others were lugging trunks. They all looked like they were drunk, but I don't think it was with liquor.

I shouldn't have worried about anyone stealing our laundry. There was too much loot in Chinatown.

I had just gotten the basket when I saw a strange red glow over Chinatown. I didn't want to go back there. Still, for Joseph's sake I thought I'd better check. So I made myself walk on.

The smell was even worse as I got close; and I was surprised to see that there was more than half of Chinatown still left. A new bonfire was blazing with about a hundred people around it, singing and carrying on like there was a party. They were watching some fifty more men and women moving about Chinatown with torches setting fire to what was left.

When all of Chinatown was burning, Captain Jack waved them back. "There may be more gunpowder in Chinatown. Retreat."

The men and women scampered toward Captain Jack as fire leaped up the sides and onto the roofs of the buildings. The flames quickly swelled bigger and bigger, until they covered every inch of wood. And then they smashed together into a huge column that rose higher and higher. The heat swept like a wave over me.

In the red light of the fire, the laughing faces seemed like strange masks; and the rock butte behind Chinatown was coated in blood.

We all jumped at the first explosion. Captain Jack had been right. There must have been kegs of gunpowder in Chinatown after all.

Another one went off, and broken boards and plates filled the air. The bits pattered against the ground when they fell like heavy raindrops.

Boom! Boom! Boom!

More sparks shot up like giant Roman candles with each new keg that went off. The crowd whooped at the fireworks.

As Chinatown blew up, a shower of sparks and burning embers rushed into the air, rising higher and higher until they could have burned the moon.

When the explosions were done, the spectators began to head back to their homes. Most of them had loot of some kind.

Seth was wearing a blue silk robe that was so long, it trailed behind him. He'd made Fred into a wheelbarrow. He held on to Fred's ankles while Fred moved on his hands. Tied to Fred's back were baskets of stuff.

It was like a game to them.

As I stood there, Miss Virginia bumped into me.

She put a hand to her throat. "Michael, you scared me."

"I'm sorry," I said. I was just about to whisper to her that we had her student and his father when I saw the basket in her arms filled with shiny silk cloth.

Suddenly I got suspicious. What was she doing here with that?

"Virginia? Virginia, where have you been?" Evie called. She came running toward us. "Father and Mother have been so worried." She stopped when she saw the basket. "Where did you get that?"

Miss Virginia looked embarrassed. "In Chinatown. It's not like anyone needed these silks anymore."

"Aren't you ashamed?" Evie demanded.

Miss Virginia defended herself. "I've done a lot for them and never got so much as a penny." She saw me staring at her. "This is my pay."

For all her high-toned talk, she wasn't any better than Seth. If that was what it meant to be respectable, then I'd be a bastard anytime.

"Michael," Evie whispered softly. She was gazing at my basket. "I expected better of you."

I shook my head frantically. "No, I didn't go into Chinatown. This is just laundry."

But Evie was already running away.

I was going to go after her to explain when I heard a wolf howl somewhere out in the wasteland. I'd plumb forgotten about the wolves.

The wolf howled again, a lean, hungry sound that turned my spine into an icicle. And I thought about the Chinese who had managed to get away. It was an even bet whether the cold would kill them before the wolves did.

At least Joseph and his father were safe in our house. Just as I was feeling relieved, Mrs. Reilly saw me and called, "Michael, have you seen any Chinese?"

I was afraid to turn around. "No'm."

"We had reports there were some of the critters sneaking around," Mrs. Duval said.

I pivoted slowly. Mrs. Reilly still had her gun, and Mrs. Duval must have fetched up hers from the street after she had finished at Ah Lee's. Mrs. Reilly was in the same clothes she'd begun with, but Mrs. Duval was now sporting a velvet waistcoat with gold buttons and a skirt of satin.

With them was Steve, decked out in a fur coat—more loot from some Chinese. And there were Jake and Johnson and diGiorgio, each of them with some fancy rig now. Seth was there too, still in his blue silk coat. They were all grinning ear to ear like cats with pails full of milk.

"I—I haven't seen anyone," I stammered.

Mrs. Duval's face was flushed—as if she had just finished dancing. Ah Lee's blood was still on her dress.

Suddenly I got the trembles real bad. I'd served them tea in our kitchen and they had drunk it like ordinary people. And that was the scary part: These murderers were our neighbors.

"Well, you tell us if you do," Mrs. Reilly said, and glanced up at the moon. The smoke had turned it a blood red. "It's going to be a hunting moon tonight."

Out in the wasteland a wolf howled like it was answering her. My shivering changed to outright shaking. I'd seen their handiwork. The wolves would have company killing tonight. But at least the wolves would be murdering for food, not for revenge.

"Are you cold, Mike?" Mrs. Duval asked sharply.

I could feel her eyes watching me like a hawk. "No'm. I mean, yes'm."

"Well, you should go home before you catch something," Mrs. Reilly said thoughtfully.

"Yes'm, I will." And I lit out of there like all of Hell was coming after me. Because it might be.

If Hell got to our house, Michael and his father wouldn't be safe.

And neither would Ma and me.

CHAPTER | 51

Joseph Young
Rock Springs
Wednesday, September 2
Dusk

Now that I knew Michael was safe, all the energy drained out of me, and I felt just like an empty sack. My legs didn't even feel like they had bones anymore. I sat down on a big overturned tub in the Purdys' basement.

"What do you think happened to White Deer and the others back at the camp?" I asked. I could already guess about Bull. Even though he had told us to leave, I was still feeling guilty about abandoning him.

"I don't know," Father murmured. "I just don't know. Poor White Deer. He thought he was going to get away." Suddenly he cradled his face in his hands, and then his shoulders began to shake. I hadn't seen him cry since Mother died.

Even though my legs still felt weak, I stumbled over to

him. "We're okay now. Maybe in a few days we'll sneak out at night and hop on a freight train and get out of here."

When he raised his head, I could see how the tears had streaked his face. "What have I gotten you into?"

I'd been scared when the mob had charged at Number Three, and I'd been even more scared at the church; but of all the things that had happened today, this was the scariest. Father always tried to find a rainbow in the worst situation.

I shifted over to a stool next him. "It's okay."

"No, it's not," he said, slapping the table in frustration. "I was stupid to chase such crazy dreams. And even stupider for dragging you along too and putting you into danger. But I was stupidest when I didn't realize how lonely I made you. I wouldn't listen to you. No, I had to be the big man spouting speeches instead. So you had to find a complete stranger to talk to. And now when I finally understand everything, it's too late." He glanced at me from the corners of his eyes. "If I hadn't been so pigheaded, we wouldn't be in this mess. I'm sorry, Joseph."

It was the first time he had ever used my Western name. I rocked back on the stool. "I never expected to hear an apology from you."

"Well, at least I can give you that much," he said bitterly.

Suddenly the ground shook. The stool I was on tipped sharply, and Father almost pitched forward onto the floor.

Things rattled all around the cellar, and an iron fell onto an overturned tub with a boom.

"What was that?" I asked. "Is it an earthquake?"

Father braced himself against the table. "The miners had gunpowder stored in their cabins in Chinatown. The flames must be setting it off."

I jumped as another explosion rocked the cellar. "Or the Patriots are blowing up Chinatown. They want to wipe us from the face of the Earth."

How could anyone hate someone so much? Their hatred seemed as huge as a mountain. How could anyone escape being crushed by something that gigantic? Suddenly I felt as cold and empty as the wasteland.

I was as foolish as Father. Maybe Bull was right: It didn't matter if I cut my hair and wore American clothes and talked like an American—America didn't want me. Only I'd cut my hair. I could never set foot in China now. China would be as deadly as America. There was no escape. I'd be as dead as the dinosaurs.

When a third explosion hit, Father's hand started to shake so badly, it worried me when I saw him reach for the scissors.

I was too terrified by the explosions to move. "Why are you doing this?" I croaked.

"I know you think I'm a useless fool. All I'm good for is making silly paper cutouts like my uncle did." When he picked up the scissors, he gripped the handles so tightly that his knuckles showed white. "But it soothes me."

"Are you making more fish?" I asked.

"No." As soon as the scissors sliced through the paper for the first time, his face calmed down.

Another explosion. More things rattled. More things fell.

However, Father's face stayed calm as he focused on the figure emerging from the paper.

I couldn't help wishing I were far away from all the explosions. Someplace safe. Like Star Rock and the lost sea and the cave of stars. Just thinking about that place now made me feel a little calmer. It was a place where peace came first. Father would have appreciated that.

He cradled the completed flower in his palm for a moment. It was one of his loveliest, with intricate petals that were as fragile as they were beautiful. And then his fingers started to curl around the flower as if he were going to crumple it up. "You're right. It's stupid to do this. I might as well wish for wings so we can fly away."

I couldn't bear to see him destroy the flower. I shot my hand out to stop him; and the sudden motion sent scraps of paper fluttering into the air. "What would you do if you weren't cutting out flowers?"

Puzzled, Father set the flower down. "I'd be quaking in my boots while I imagined all the horrible things the Western miners are going to do to us."

I ran my hand through my hair, feeling the short hairs

where there used to be a queue. "Isn't that just what they want: for us to shake like mice while we wait to die?"

"We could talk if you like."

"About what?" I laughed. "About how stupid we've both been? I think we can take that for granted. Instead of counting all our mistakes, spend your last moments doing what makes you happy."

"You said cutouts were old-fashioned," Father teased. At least I had made him smile a little.

"I still think they are." I shrugged. "But look at what being modern got me."

"It's also Chinese," Father said, "not American."

"Maybe it's time for me to learn more of that, too," I said.

"I used to think this was silly when I saw my uncle doing it." Father picked up another sheet. "I thought it was just purely decorative."

"Well, you're making flowers, after all," I said, puzzled.

He smiled. "No, I'm going to drive some ghosts from this house."

"What do you mean?" I asked.

"I know something about dreams," he said wistfully, "and the saddest thing in the world is a dream that's only half born. When he died, my uncle left a path for the railroads; maybe I can do this much."

I recognized the beginning of patterned wings. "It's a butterfly."

"To appreciate the flower." Father smiled. "There's a whole garden of them sketched on the walls of this house. They're dreams that have never become real. And if dreams aren't allowed to become real, then all they can be are ghosts."

Suddenly I understood, and I reached for the other pair of scissors. "I can't do the fancy stuff like you."

Father slid a sheet over to me. "We'll start you out on some simple shapes. You'll learn to do the more intricate designs later." He stopped when he realized we might not have a "later."

I wasn't going to let him have enough time to feel sad.

"Let's enjoy what time we have," I said, and began to cut out a tulip.

CHAPTER | 52

Michael Purdy
Rock Springs
Wednesday, September 2
Dusk

Ma must have been watching for me from the parlor, because she opened the front door as soon as she saw me. "Get in, Michael," she said, waving to me.

I stepped through the front door, dirty shoes and all.

She let her breath out in a rush. "Thank Heaven you're all right."

"For now," I said, "but Mrs. Reilly and Mrs. Duval are still on the prowl."

She sighed. "Well, our guests should be safe inside here."

"How are they?" I asked.

"I guess they're fine." Ma shrugged. "Not a peep from them. They won't even let me look downstairs."

I glanced around nervously and asked in a low voice, "So what do we do with them?"

Ma ran a hand through her hair. I hadn't noticed before: Some of it was gray. "We'll hide them until the fuss dies down a bit. Then maybe we can sneak them onto a train some night. With any luck we can get them to someplace safe— though there don't seem many places like that nowadays."

I touched the gray hair on the sides of her head. "I'm sorry, Ma. Did I put some more gray hairs there?"

Ma knew the spot I was touching. I guess she had studied it in a mirror. "None of the hair's your doing. That's just what comes of living."

"I'm still sorry," I said. "But . . ." I hesitated.

"What?" Ma asked.

I knew I'd lose my courage if I didn't blurt it out. "Why didn't Pa stay with us?"

Ma glanced at the watch on the wall. "Let him rest in peace."

"But I have to know," I said urgently. "Was . . . was it my fault?"

Ma looked startled. "Land, no. What put that into your head? He was the happiest man alive when you were born."

"Then why did he keep going away ?" I asked.

Ma's face softened. "I guess you're old enough." But I think she didn't want to remember. She looked as if there were old wounds that still hadn't healed. "He was too sweet for his own good. He didn't have much backbone. He hadn't been able to say no when his family wanted him to marry this rich girl. But they never loved one another. He talked about getting a divorce, but he didn't seem to have the nerve."

"So he didn't care what happened to us?" I asked angrily.

Ma defended him even now. "He saw to it that we had this house, and he would have come around in the end, but he died before that could happen."

"So all you have left of him is the house and the watch and the notebooks," I said. It wasn't much of a trade.

"I have you," Ma said.

"But I'm the reason folks treat you the way they do," I said miserably. "If I wasn't around, they might have forgotten."

Ma took my shoulders and gave me a little shake. "Whatever put that notion into your head? I love you, Michael." Her eyes studied my surprised face. "I guess I'm just a mite out of practice saying it, and I'm sorry."

I didn't know what to say for a while. I was just so happy to have been wrong. "I reckon we both wasted a lot of time." And then I turned toward my bed. "Can I show you something?"

"It's been a long day and I'm tired," Ma said, but then she saw how disappointed I was. "Well, what is it?"

"Remember I told you how Joseph and I found fossils and bones?" Since she knew about Joseph, I didn't see the harm anymore in getting out the box. "Joseph and I have been digging these up." Then I got out the notebook I had been using and flipped to my pages. "See? I kept a record. I even found dinosaur bones like Pa used to."

"You really are your pa's son," Ma said. Thoughtfully she turned the pages one by one, as if remembering.

She looked so sad that I took out my first shell—the one that Joseph had given me. "This is from when this was an old ocean. But don't it shine like a star?"

Ma held it up and studied it. "Like it's a star that fell from the sky." Raising it, she closed her eyes. Her lips moved silently as if she was making a wish on it.

So I commenced to wish too: wanting to whisk us all to Star Rock, where we'd be safe from wolves—the ones with two legs as well as the ones with four.

CHAPTER | 53

Joseph Young
Rock Springs
Wednesday, September 2
After sundown

The Purdys looked upset when we popped up out of the basement.

"Maybe we'd better go back downstairs," I said to Father.

However, Father seemed more determined than ever. He started for the parlor with his tub with the flowers inside, hidden beneath a towel. *"It won't take long,"* he promised. He was already heading into the parlor. *"Do you have some paste?"*

Alarmed, Mrs. Purdy stepped in front of him. *"I don't what you're planning, but this isn't the time."*

Father held his ground. *"You've been such good friends. And we have no other way to thank you."*

"You can thank us by hiding in the basement again," Mrs. Purdy insisted.

"We may not have another chance," Father insisted.

"To do what?" Mrs. Purdy demanded.

Father hugged the tub against his stomach. *"I can't tell you. That would ruin the surprise."*

Michael nodded to the tub. *"Ma, he wants to give you a gift."*

Mrs. Purdy fiddled with her collar nervously. *"It's not like we get any presents. But why did he have to pick now?"*

"Please let us do this one thing," Father coaxed, *"and then I promise, we won't budge from your basement."*

Mrs. Purdy put her hands on her hips. *"If you aren't the most exasperating man,"* she said—which was certainly true enough.

Michael disappeared into the parlor. Through the doorway, I saw him peeking through a curtain into the street. *"The coast is clear,"* he called.

Mrs. Purdy stepped to the side. *"Michael, get some flour and water. You'll have to make paste for our guests."*

Michael and I got the paste together quickly. *"What's your pa cooking up, anyway?"* he asked.

I shrugged. *"I don't know, but he says it's important."*

"This is crazy," he said.

"Yes," I agreed, *"but then so is the whole world today."*

When I brought the big pot of paste from the kitchen and two knives, I saw that Father had closed the door. He opened it at my tap. "Hurry," he said in Chinese.

I didn't need his urging. As soon as I had slipped through, he shut the door. He had already begun to take the flowers out of the tub and lay them along the floor. "We can't put the garden outside, so we'll have to put it inside."

I never thought I would enjoy spending any time with Father; and yet here I was pasting cutouts on the walls with him.

As the big gold watch ticked faintly on the wall, Father and I ringed the parlor with flowers and butterflies and birds. I felt the ghosts leave the room, leaving it bright and colorful. How long had it been since I had seen anything like this? Not since San Francisco. If Michael had been born here, he had probably never seen it.

Suddenly I began to feel good inside—like I did at Star Rock.

We had worked as quickly as we could, but Mrs. Purdy began to get impatient. When the watch began chiming, she opened the door. *"It's been an hour. You've got to go back down."*

CHAPTER | 54

Ma had been all set to scold them. I know because she had been rehearsing the speech out loud while we had been waiting; and it wasn't one I would have wanted aimed at me. However, when she entered the parlor, she halted dead in her tracks.

I followed on her heels and stopped too. Magic had changed the room from drab, unpainted boards into all the gardens I had ever read about—with all sorts of brightly colored flowers and even butterflies and birds.

Joseph glanced at Pa's watch on the wall. "I'm sorry. I didn't realize that it was that late."

Mr. Young was just as shocked. "I guess we lost track of time."

"Oh, my," Ma said. "Oh, my," she said again. All that fretting had flown right out of her head.

"We would have put the garden outside if we could," Mr. Young explained. "But for obvious reasons, we can't."

"It's just like I—" Ma began, and then shook her head. "No, I never dreamed anything like this. It's a jungle of flowers."

Neither had I. I turned in a slow circle. I hardly noticed the outline of the mantel and other drawings. Mostly I looked at the flowers. It's funny, but I felt like the ghosts were gone.

"Is this what San Francisco's like?" I asked Joseph.

"Even better," he said. "But these flowers don't have any scent."

"They'll last longer though," I said.

I reckon someone with a real garden would have laughed at Ma and me. They hadn't grown up in a wasteland where even the water will make you sick and most everything is ugly browns and grays. I'd never known what it was like to be surrounded by colors.

Mr. Young scratched his head, embarrassed. "It's not much of a way to say thank you."

"It's us who should thank you," Ma said, and began to cry.

CHAPTER | 55

Joseph Young
Rock Springs
Wednesday, September 2
Evening

"*B*ut my real gift to you is to leave," Father said to the
Purdys. "*I just wanted to leave you something to remember
me by. It'll be easier to hide just one person.*" He turned to
me. "*So Joseph, you stay with them.*"

Father seemed like such a gentle dreamer, but he was
really strong inside. He was like a river that seemed calm on
the surface but had powerful currents underneath. I had
never understood just how brave Father was. He hadn't
been a coward those other times when he had refused to
defend himself with his fists. He'd been trying to stay true
to his dreams.

"But you can't," I said, suddenly frightened. The mob
would kill Father. I tried to think of life without him; and
I just couldn't, wouldn't.

Father shrugged. "Don't worry. We otters are slippery

fellows. I'll get away and find you again. It will be less dangerous for our hosts to hide one person rather than two."

I bet he had come up with that wild notion down in the basement. No wonder he had been so set on making the flowers. He must have thought it would be the last thing we would do together. "But you never have any luck," I protested.

Father smiled sadly. "I haven't been much of a father. You said it yourself: I got you into this mess. Let me get you out of it."

"I'm going with you," I insisted.

"Don't argue," he said.

I felt this terrible ache inside when I thought of life without him. "But I need you," I said.

I was going to argue more when someone began to bang at the front door.

"*Mary, may we come in?*" a woman called.

CHAPTER | 56

Michael Purdy
Rock Springs
Wednesday, September 2
Evening

I just about dropped dead when I heard Mrs. Reilly knock.

It was a good thing that Ma had a clear head. "Mike, don't open the door yet." Wiping her eyes, she spun around and hooked one arm through one of Mr. Young's and the other with Joseph. "You're not going anywhere but the cellar."

"Let me go out the back door. I'll get them to chase me. Just hide Joseph," Mr. Young begged, trying to tug free.

But years of washing dirty laundry had made Ma as strong as any miner. "We sink or swim together." And she commenced hauling them both from the parlor and through her bedroom and into the kitchen.

"Mary, yoo-hoo, Mary. Are you in?" From the cheerful way Mrs. Reilly sounded, you would have figured she was paying a social call.

The doorknob started to turn. Quickly I flung myself against it to hold it shut. "Wait, Mrs. Reilly. I ain't dressed," I fibbed.

Through the open doorways, I saw Ma practically throw our guests down the cellar stairs.

Then, locking the door so they couldn't get out, Ma whipped around. Straightening her apron, she strode toward me. And with each step, she grew taller and more determined—even though she knew Hell was coming straight at us.

Right at that moment, I wouldn't have traded her for a dozen pillowy mas. A pillow ma would have blubbered like a crybaby and gotten us all killed. The ma I needed was exactly the one who motioned me to get out of her way.

When she flung the door open, the stench blew inside the house. I saw Mrs. Duval standing hip to hip with Mrs. Reilly, and behind them were Seth, Steve, Jake, Johnson, and diGiorgio. Ash floated around their heads like snowflakes.

It must have been a strain, but Ma managed a friendly smile. "Land! What you doing out at this time of night?"

Mrs. Duval stared at Ma like she was made out of glass and she could see right through her. "We've been doing what we should. What about you, Mary?"

Ma placed a hand beneath her throat and laughed nervously. "Me, why I've just been spending a quiet night at home."

Mrs. Reilly nudged Mrs. Duval proudly. "Well, this hawk-eye here killed two of the Chinese with just three shots."

Mrs. Duval poked an elbow in her friend's ribs. "I hear you got two yourself, Emma."

Mrs. Reilly beamed. "Ain't you the kind one, Justine."

"And you would have had three," Mrs. Duval said, pretty as you please, "but I hear somebody threw off your aim and you only winged the rascal in the leg."

Mrs. Reilly tossed her head back proudly. "Well, we learned them a lesson they'll never forget. Those that can still run won't stop until they're out of the territory."

I nearly gagged thinking about their schooling. Ma's eyes flicked down to the bloodstains on Mrs. Duval's dress. Ma had done enough laundry to recognize blood. Carefully she looked up at Mrs. Duval's face again. "I see," Ma said softly.

"May we come in?" Mrs. Duval asked. She started to push her way in. "We've come to invite you to our soiree."

Throwing her arm across the doorway, Ma shook her head. "Not in that condition, Justine."

Mrs. Reilly frowned. "Don't tell me you're taking the Chinese's side, Mary?"

Ma stood like a rock. "I admit you've got a list of fair grievances, but that's no excuse for what happened today."

Mrs. Duval leaned her head to the side like a bird. "Were we just supposed to roll over and let them do whatever they want?"

"There's the law," Ma said.

"Hang the law. The Company owns the courts," Mrs. Duval snapped.

"I meant the Lord's law," Ma corrected her. "We all have to answer to Him."

"You're a fine one to talk about the Commandments," Mrs. Duval sniffed. "Most respectable folk would never give you the time of day, but I've always stuck up for you. And this is the thanks I get?"

Mrs. Reilly put a hand on Mrs. Duval's shoulder. "We ain't got time to jaw about the past, Justine. We still got work to do." And then she looked over Mrs. Duval at Ma. "I'll have my say here. We come to have you join us, Mary."

"You seem to be doing well enough without me," Ma said.

"You got it wrong, Mary," Mrs. Duval's voice got sharp as a knife's edge. "This isn't an invitation. I told you before: You're either with us or against us."

"In other words, you want me to bloody my hands too," Ma snapped.

Mrs. Duval's one thick eyebrow got close to her eyes as she narrowed them. "You can't just sit back and profit from our hard work."

I wanted to warn Ma not to cross them, but Ma spoke her mind as usual. "Work, is it? Is that what they're calling butchery nowadays? So how much do you get paid per head?"

"The hard part's done now, Mary," Mrs. Reilly coaxed. "You don't have to touch a pistol. Just come and help us look. We've sent out groups to sweep the camps, and the rest of us are clearing out the town."

Ma raised her eyebrows. "Look for what? You just boasted you'd chased all the Chinese out of the territory."

Mrs. Duval shrugged. "Those Chinese are natural-born thieves. They could have snuck in any house without folks noticing. So we're searching all of them—including yours."

"I'll handle any unwanted visitors myself," Ma insisted.

Mrs. Duval stared at Ma hard. "You wouldn't be hiding anyone, would you?"

Ma laughed. "Now what reason do I have to love Chinese?" I was surprised at how good she was at fibbing.

Mrs. Reilly poked Mrs. Duval. "Come on. You've heard her often enough."

Mrs. Duval continued to stare at Ma. "We're going after the Chinese lovers as well as the Chinese," she warned. She rattled off a bunch a names. Most of them were with the mining company or the railroad or were like Mr. Kincaid and dealt with the Chinese in some way.

"My, my, you've got quite a list there." Ma fixed her eyes on Mrs. Duval. "Someone's been busy planning, hasn't she?"

"We've had our noses rubbed in the dirt for a long time," Mrs. Duval said. "We don't forget."

Mrs. Reilly lowered her voice. "You ought to cooperate, Mary. You don't want to give folks the wrong idea."

Ma folded her arms defiantly. "And you're the one who decides what's right and what's wrong? Who else is on your list? People with left hands? People with blue eyes? Where does it stop?"

"Now, Mary, we've been friends for a long time." Mrs. Reilly tried to soothe her.

"You already said we weren't friends anymore. So get out." Ma jerked her head at the street.

Mrs. Reilly suddenly craned her neck to look beyond Ma. "What did you do to your parlor?"

Ma shoved some hair from her forehead. "I finally did some decorating."

Mrs. Reilly's eyes widened. "It's beautiful."

Mrs. Duval squinted at Ma. "That's not like you, Mary."

The notion bothered Mrs. Reilly too. "No, it ain't."

Mrs. Duval stared at Ma suspiciously, like she was already aiming at Ma over a gun barrel. "What's going on here, Mary?"

"You're . . . not welcome in here," Ma said nervously.

Steve came up behind Mrs. Reilly and Mrs. Duval. "I think we'd better take a look-see in there."

"This is America," Ma protested. "You can't just charge into a person's house."

Our friends were going to be as dead as Ah Lee. And maybe so were we—unless I did something. Muscle wasn't going to work—not against that whole pack. So we couldn't keep them out if they wanted to come in. Desperately I tried to think of a plan.

Mrs. Reilly and Mrs. Duval stepped back into the street

to make way for Steve. "We're coming in," Steve swore.

It was not like Seth to be patient. He bulled past Steve and gave Ma a shove. "Out of the way!"

"Seth, behave yourself," Mrs. Reilly snapped.

After all that she had done, it seemed odd for a human wolf like her to think about manners at a time like this. And then I recollected what Ma had said—that Mrs. Reilly didn't think of us as the enemy. With her friends she liked to have manners. And she had always felt guilty whenever her boy beat me up.

And suddenly I had a handle on things. I didn't know what would happen to me; but I had to protect Ma and my friends.

"Don't you touch my ma," I shouted at Seth, and rushed toward him.

Seth was so surprised, my charge knocked us both past Steve and out through the doorway and onto the street.

"This is my house. My house. My house!" I said. I had ahold of his collar as he stumbled and fell backward with me on top.

I wasn't a fighter and never would be. But I was mad and scared, so somehow that turned me into a human windmill. On any other night Seth could have outboxed me. But I made up in desperation for what I missed in science. And for every punch he landed, I hit him with three.

"Stop, stop," he began to scream.

I was winning! I was winning! Why hadn't I done this before!

"You let my Seth go," Mrs. Reilly said. She tried to grab me, but I stayed put. I'd never felt so strong. Every insult—every wrong—I was going to pay my enemy back double.

"Stop him, Steve," Mrs. Reilly ordered frantically.

I guess Steve reckoned I was crazy. I certainly must have looked the picture. "Well . . ." Steve said, hanging back.

"Somebody do something," Mrs. Reilly said angrily.

All my enemies were too scared of me. Enemies. Here I was doing the same thing as them. I guess I couldn't judge Mrs. Reilly after all. I guess nobody could.

Worse, I realized just how dumb I was. I'd win the fight but cost us our lives. After all, I'd started the fight just so I could lose it.

The trouble was that Seth had given up fighting. He was holding up his hands in front of his face while he begged for help.

"Fight me," I told him. "Fight me."

He kept huddling, though, so I couldn't figure out what to do. And then Ma shouted, "Michael, stop that."

That gave me my excuse. I turned to look over my shoulder. "But—" I began.

And as I knew he would, Seth snuck a punch. As punches went, it wasn't much compared to his others. However, I keeled over backward like it was a real haymaker.

"I'll teach you, you bastard!" Seth yelled.

I wanted to get up and defend myself; but I made myself lie there, telling myself, This is for Joseph. This is for your ma. If I beat Seth, a riled-up Mrs. Reilly would keep on foaming like a wolf. She'd ransack our house until she found our friends.

But a guilty Mrs. Reilly was another thing. Chinese and Chinese lovers were fair game; but I was gambling that she'd wind up remembering the old days and seeing us different.

So I had to be as brave as Ma.

Seth worked me over pretty good with his feet until I was ready to tell him to stop. The only problem was that it hurt so much to breathe now that I couldn't talk.

"Seth will kill him, Emma," Ma pleaded.

As I lay in pain, I wondered if I'd really turn into a ghost this time. But if I could take their minds off the search, it didn't matter.

"Stop it, Seth," Mrs. Reilly hollered. And when Seth went right on kicking, she said, "Give me a hand, Steve."

And suddenly the beating stopped. It hurt to open my eyes, but I saw Steve had grabbed hold of Seth.

Ma knelt beside me. "Are you all right, Mike?"

"It . . . hurts . . . to . . . breathe," I said.

Mrs. Reilly was biting her lip. "Somebody fetch a doctor."

"I think we've had enough company for one night," Ma said. She whispered to me. "Can you stand up on your own?"

I nodded. With Ma's help, I rose.

It was just like I thought. Mrs. Reilly was looking embarrassed over the whipping Seth had given me.

Mrs. Reilly made a noise in the back of her throat.

"Seth didn't really mean it."

Ma supported me with her arm. "Then maybe you should leave us alone."

"But—" Mrs. Duval started to object.

"Haven't you done enough to us?" Ma snapped.

Mrs. Duval looked like she was going to get back up on her soapbox, but Mrs. Reilly jerked her head. "Let's go."

"But we still have to search their house," Mrs. Duval objected.

"Privacy is a small enough pleasure," Ma said. "And you want to take even that away from us. Are we next on your list?"

Mrs. Reilly looked ashamed. "Of course not. You're not Chinese."

Ma wrapped her arms around me. "But our parlor's different from yours. And we're different too. We're not respectable. Don't you want to kill us, too?"

Mrs. Reilly held up her hands, embarrassed. "Don't carry on so, Mary."

Ma begged her former friend. "For Heaven's sake, stop this madness, Emma. Stop it now!"

Mrs. Reilly took a deep breath and then let it go in a shaky, tired sort of way. And with that breath went every ounce of wolf. "I'm sorry, Mary," she said.

It was like Ma had said. Mrs. Reilly was a decent-enough woman if she thought you were her own kind. "Mary's right. Let's call it a day."

"But—" Mrs. Duval said.

"We're all tired." Mrs. Reilly shook her head. "And I've got my boy to tend to."

I took some satisfaction in the fact that Seth's face looked as bad as mine felt.

Ma helped me as far as the door. We both turned when we got there. The human pack of wolves was splitting up and heading for home.

I'd done it!

CHAPTER | 57

Joseph Young
Rock Springs
Monday, September 7
Morning

Father and I stayed in the cellar during the day while Mrs. Purdy did her laundry down there.

Mrs. Purdy wanted us just to relax while she worked, saying that we were guests. However, neither Father nor I were used to being idle, so we pitched in. Father said it would be good practice when we went to work with Uncle Bright Star.

Laundry was almost as hard work as the mines; but I had fun because of Michael. We splashed each other so much that his exasperated mother said the only clothes we were washing were the ones we were wearing.

In the evenings Father and I snuck up to the parlor to play card games with the Purdys in the dream garden. I hadn't thought about it before, but Mrs. Purdy must have been as much an outcast as her son. And my father. And me.

Father and Mrs. Purdy both seemed to sense they had the same kind of courage—and stubbornness—because they became friendly. So Michael and I could feel free to leave them alone. While they chatted or played cards, Michael and I would lie on the floor and look through his father's notebooks. We'd both have to keep notes like that when we went to college and studied fossils. But it was as if we had just dropped by like real visitors to spend the evening.

Mrs. Purdy would go out to scout. Even at night the Patriots were keeping an eye on the railroad tracks, still determined to kill off any Chinese they had missed.

And the news she heard was terrible: Some of the Chinese who had fled into the wasteland had died from the cold or, worse, the wolves. And all over the Territory, Chinese were being killed or chased out of all the Chinatowns. The Patriots had started off a new chain of slaughter in the west. I felt guilty for enjoying myself with the Purdys.

CHAPTER | 58

Michael Purdy
Rock Springs
Tuesday, September 8
Afternoon

Ma started to spend her spare time in the parlor, her in a chair that she dragged from the kitchen and me in my bed because I was still mending. There were no bones broke, but I felt like one big bruise.

The funny thing was that I didn't have to go to Star Rock to feel good anymore.

"The garden's pretty, Ma, ain't it?" I said. Next to Star Rock, it was my favoritest thing.

"It is, at that, Mike," Ma agreed, "but I'm thinking you ought to see real ones."

"I don't know if you can grow one outside here," I warned.

"Outside that door ain't the only place for a garden," Ma said. "There's a lot better places than here where flowers grow."

I just stared. "You mean leave here?"

"It's wrong to hold on to memories, and that's all this house is," Ma said, and gazed at the room. "I should have realized that a long time ago. This is no place for you. It's no place for me, either. I'm tired of ghosts, aren't you? Not just here but all around the town. It's all those old ghosts of past wrongs just haunting folks and driving them on like they're possessed."

I just stared. "But you said we don't have the money to go."

On the wall, the big gold watch chimed. "Between the house and that, we would," Ma said.

"That's Pa's," I protested. "I got his notebooks to take with me. But what have you got?"

"I've got you," she said; and when she smiled, she looked a lot like the girl in that photograph.

CHAPTER | 59

Joseph Young
Rock Springs
Wednesday, September 9
Morning

Suddenly one morning I woke to the ringing of a bell—though I couldn't say if it was a church's or a locomotive's. Peeking out of the basement, we saw it was dawn. Mrs. Purdy came by, draping a shawl over her shoulders. *"I'll go see what the ruckus is all about."*

"Be careful," Michael said, worried.

"Don't fret." She winked at him.

When she came back, she looked sad, so at first I thought it was bad news. But she said the soldiers had come.

So it was good news . . . but also bad news. I felt almost as sad. *"So, I guess it's safe for us to leave here."*

Mrs. Purdy clapped her hands together. *"You're not going anywhere until you've had breakfast."*

We had our last meal together, but we didn't talk much.

Who knew where any of us would wind up? When we were done, Father cleared his throat. *"I guess we better leave."*

"Where are you going to go?" Mrs. Purdy asked.

"I'll find work in some other Chinatown," Father said. *"We have friends in San Francisco."*

"Are you sure?" I asked in Chinese. I doubted if we'd be welcome there. There were still a lot of Chinese who blamed Father for losing the fight against the new laws.

"We'll be safe with Sean until we figure out what to do," Father said. "My pride almost got us killed." Then he smiled at Mrs. Purdy. *"We'd better sneak out the back way so no one will know what house we hid in."*

Mrs. Purdy shook her head. *"You're guests. You'll use the front door."*

"But what if someone sees us?" Father protested.

"I don't care what anyone thinks. We ain't staying. I won't abide a place where this can happen." She glanced toward the parlor. *"Though I hate to leave the garden when I just got it."*

I looked at her in surprise. *"Have you picked out a destination?"*

"It depends on how much we get for the house and a watch." Mrs. Purdy shrugged. *"But I think someplace by the water."*

"Think about San Francisco," Father suggested. *"And in the meantime you can reach us care of either of these friends."* He wrote down the addresses of Uncle Bright Star's laundry as well as Uncle Sean's house.

The chairs scraped on the floor as we got up. I hated

to leave this house as much as I had once hated to leave San Francisco. My special friend was here, and we'd been happy for a few days.

"Wait a moment," Michael said. He disappeared into the parlor and came back with a box. It was the shells. *"Here."*

I shook my head. *"They're yours."*

"You lost yours back at the camp," Michael said, shoving it into my hands. *"And you won't be able to get any more."*

"If you're leaving, neither will you," I pointed out.

"Split them," Father suggested. So that was what we did. The trouble was that we each kept trying to give each other the best pieces. And as we argued, I also felt better. If there was a lot of hatred in the outside, there were also people like the Purdys.

The biggest fight was over the shell I had first given him. *"No, I want you to have it,"* he said. *"It's just like a wishing star."*

I said, *"Then you'll need it."*

"You'll need it more," he insisted. Suddenly he grinned. *"I already got all my wishes."*

"It's as important to know how to receive as to give a gift," Father said in Chinese.

I decided that I shouldn't refuse anything that might grant a wish; but as I took it, I smiled at Michael. *"You know, Star Rock isn't a place you go to."*

"It's a place you make," he agreed.

When we left through the front door, people stared.

"Good-bye and good luck," Michael and Mrs. Purdy called and waved at us. After that display of hospitality, I hoped they would leave soon.

As we walked toward the troops, Father felt the back of my head. "When I get a chance, I'll give you a trim. If you're going to have short hair, we should make it look more like a Westerner's."

"For better or worse, America's our home," I said.

Father arched an eyebrow. "But you're still Chinese too."

"Yes," I said, matching him stride for stride. "I know it now."

CHAPTER | 60

Michael Purdy
Rock Springs
Thursday, September 10
Afternoon

The funny thing was that we got to leave Rock Springs before Joseph and his father did.

The Company lied to the Chinese miners who had made it to other towns in the Territory. The Company told them that they were getting a free ride to California and packed them on a train at night. When the train came to a stop, the Chinese were back in Rock Springs. And the heartless Company wouldn't let them leave, so Joseph and his father were stuck with everyone else.

There was one mine where Americans and Chinese had gone on working with one another; but even those Chinese wanted to leave now.

Though the governor had sent in enough soldiers to fight a war, they didn't have much stomach for the duty and gave the Chinese almost as many dirty looks as the Patriots did.

The Patriots strutted around like they still owned the town, boasting that there wasn't a jury in the Territory that would convict them.

Before they took it into their heads to do something to us, too, Ma sold the watch to Mr. Kincaid, who'd managed to dodge the Patriots that terrible day.

Then we packed up. I had just the notebook and the fossils and one of the paper flowers I managed to peel off the wall. Ma didn't have much besides her photograph, so we did it quick.

I was moving so slow because of the bruises that Ma commenced to have second thoughts. "Maybe we should wait until your bruises heal."

"I'd leave this town if I only had one leg and had to hop," I swore.

When we left the house, Ma closed the door and then stared straight ahead. "Don't look back, Mike," she said.

And I didn't. I was leaving all that haunting and ghost stuff behind.

I wasn't a ghost in town, either. For the first time in my life I felt like folks saw me. As we walked toward the station, heads turned. I guess word had gotten around about what we'd done. Most folks looked real ashamed. I got the feeling that by now decent folk agreed that we had done the right thing. Even if they still didn't like the Chinese, they figured things had gone too far. I think they would have even said something to us if they hadn't been afraid of the Patriots.

Then Steve sidled out of a saloon and glared at us; but he didn't have the sand to do anything until Jake, Johnson, and diGiorgio crawled out of an alley. Folks skedaddled from the street like a bomb had gone off. No one wanted to cross them.

I reckon the Patriots are right about a jury. Even if folks thought the Patriots were guilty as sin, they'd be too scared to vote that way.

Steve seemed to know that too. Now that he had a pack behind him, he got pretty bold. "Go on, leave, you traitors!" he snarled, and commenced to growl and bark insults and threats you wouldn't have laid on a mangy dog.

I started to get pretty scared, and even though it hurt, I started to hurry along; but Ma called softly from behind me. "Walk, Mike. We might be leaving town, but we done nothing to be ashamed of."

And didn't Ma look grand? Just strolling along as if Steve and his mob were just so many flies buzzing around. I reckon Ma had lived her whole life that way.

And I recollected how folks in this town had been saying mean things to me all my life, so why should my last hour here be any different? I did my best to walk like I was the king of the May and didn't have a care in the world—which wasn't all that easy.

Bad as Steve was, I was really scared Mrs. Duval would pop out. She was deadlier than any Patriot, and I was glad she didn't show before we reached the station.

Steve didn't stop there, but at least the soldiers were around. I glued myself to a big, broad sergeant, figuring that if the Patriots shot off a gun, it was more likely to hit him than me.

Ma got two tickets to Denver, which was as far as we could afford; but we figured we'd work our way west from there until we ran out of land. In the meantime I tried to catch a glimpse of the boxcars where the Chinese were being forced to live; but I couldn't see Joseph or his father.

"Michael," I heard Miss Evie call. I turned to see her walking toward me with a basket on her arm. "Thank Heaven I caught you. I heard you were leaving." She held out the basket to Ma. "You must be Mrs. Purdy. I made a lunch for you."

Ma took it. "That's right kind of you," she said, taking it.

Miss Evie's cheeks were a bright red when she turned to me. "Michael, I'm sorry for the things I said that night. I wish I'd done what you and your mother did. A lot of other people wish they had too." She glanced at Steve. "They're just too afraid to say it in front of those yahoos."

"Why, thank you, Miss Evie," I said.

Suddenly she lunged forward. "I'll . . . I'll miss you," she said; and before I could stop her, she kissed my cheek on the one part that wasn't bruised. Then, spinning around, she dashed away.

Ma bounced up and down on the balls of her feet. "My, my, Mike. Still want to leave?"

The Patriots were glaring at Miss Evie as she passed. She ignored them, keeping her head up high.

That had taken more courage than what I had done. I was leaving. She was staying.

"No, there's no place for us here now," I said. "I want to see the ocean. The real one." I looked off toward our special place. "I just wish it had been safe enough to show you Star Rock."

Ma put a hand on my shoulder. After the massacre we had gone back to not hugging much, and that small touch meant a lot.

"We'll find other places, Mike," she promised.

And I knew we would. Together.

CHAPTER | 61

Joseph Young
San Francisco
Tuesday, December 8
Morning

We might still be trapped in Rock Springs if it weren't for Father. None of the Chinese wanted to stay. We had no money or tools, and the only clothes we had were on our backs. But the Company wouldn't let us go. They wouldn't even pay us our back wages so we could leave.

The head man himself, Ah Say, had been wounded and had crawled miles to safety. Ah Koon had had to give the Patriots all his money and his fur coat too; but he had saved his skin as well. Now they were too scared to even peep.

We all met outside the boxcars we were using as the village until the new Chinatown got built. There were a lot of crazy notions tossed out—from walking thousands of miles on our own to petitioning the Manchu emperor to help (as if the Manchus cared what happened to

Chinese in the Land of the Golden Mountain). As the schemes got wilder and wilder, I started fingering the shell in my pocket and hoping it was a real wishing star.

Finally White Deer stood up—he'd listened to his dream and left the mines and camp early with a blanket and warm clothes. Spinner had survived the massacre too; but the rest of our cabin would no longer be sending money back to their families. Neither James, Paul, nor Thomas had survived. Bull didn't live either, and Father and I talked about sending some money to his family too.

At that moment White Deer's simple, calm manner was a sharp contrast to all the bombast of the previous speakers. "If you want to know what to do," White Deer suggested, "ask Otter. He's had a lot of experience." And he pointed at Father.

Of course, everyone knew Father's reputation, so there were groans and jeers at that.

The insults washed off Father as they always did. Rising to his feet, he faced his hecklers. "Whatever you think of me, America is still a land of laws, and what the Company is doing is illegal. They have no right to keep us."

One of the younger miners sneered, "Sit down, Fish Man. You told us the same thing about that other American law, and they still went ahead and passed it." And there were a lot of contemptuous nods.

I thought Father would crumple up like a paper flower. I know I would have under all that scorn.

"I don't blame you for not trusting me," Father admitted. "But who else was there when we made the paths for the trains?" Hands went up all through the crowd.

"Get to the point, Fish Man," the young heckler said.

"I will," Father said as he nodded to a gray-haired miner with his hand up. "But first tell them, classmate. Tell these others what we went through when we built the railroad."

The gray-haired miner growled, "It was a lot more dangerous than here."

"Nothing's more deadly than here," the heckler insisted.

The gray-haired miner shot back, "When we worked on the railroad, you could die a dozen different ways every day. It was like being in a war. One out of every ten men died. And that doesn't count all the ones who got maimed."

Father jerked his head at the old miner. "Classmate, tell him what the winter in the mountains was like."

The gray-haired miner raised a hand over his head. "We had the worst blizzards of the century. We had to live under the snow and walk through tunnels. We worked longer hours for less pay than here. I lost a brother to the cold. A cousin lost his toes to frostbite."

There were about thirty of Father's classmates, and they chimed in with so many other horror stories that the heckler and the other young miners, who hadn't been on the railroad, held their tongues.

Then, to my amazement, Father took off his shirt. He hated people to see his back, so I knew what it cost him to do so. Slowly he pivoted so everyone could see his mysterious scars. "A lot of you have been curious about how I got these. Well, this is what happened when I got fed up and tried to leave. The railroad whipped me like a slave to make me stay. But a whipping isn't going to stop me this time. I'm a free man and so is my boy. I don't care if their whips strip my back to the bare bone. I'm taking my son away from here."

I just stared. I supposed if I'd been tortured, I wouldn't want to relive the memory either. But I wish he had told me. Maybe things would have been different—though knowing me, maybe not. I decided then and there that I couldn't control the past, but I could do something about the future.

The older miners began to murmur to one another, and then the gray-haired miner stood up. "I'm with you, classmate."

"So am I," said another miner. "Let's teach these young ones what it really means to be tough."

And then all the old railroad men got to their feet. Were they fossils? Yes. But that made them hard as the mountains themselves. And Father shone like one of the stars of Star Rock.

One by one the younger miners got up as well. I just sat there stunned, and so I was one of the last. It was White Deer who leaned over and whispered, "Aren't you going to get up, boy?"

I rose sheepishly to join the others.

Father himself said that if the other miners hadn't been so frightened and desperate, they wouldn't have listened to him any more than they had before.

The Company thought they held all the cards; but they had never played poker with Father. For most of his life he'd been organizing people and fighting for hopeless causes.

At first we tried all sorts of peaceful, legal ways to win our freedom—reasoning and then pleading, but the Company turned deaf ears to us.

Those were busy times for him and me; and I worked that wishing star overtime. When the Company still refused, Father finally talked the Chinese into going on strike. That was a hard choice for most, because it meant there would be no money for their families, and it's bred into guests to send cash back home.

It took all Father's skill and the loyalty of his classmates to hold the strike together. When the Company reopened the mines on September 12, only a quarter of the Chinese went.

But a few days later the Company cut off our supplies. Even though we bought our own food, we had to depend upon the Company to bring it to us. And so most of the others gave in.

However, there were forty guests—mostly his classmates from the railroad, but also White Deer and Spinner—who listened to Father. And finally it was the Company that caved in! We stuck in their throats like fishbones, until it was cheaper and easier to spit out the troublemakers. And they decided to gradually let the others go too as they brought in replacements.

Father and I rode the train back to San Francisco with the other miners, who treated us like their champions. No one called him the Fish Man anymore. They called him the Dragon Man because he'd passed through his gate. And I was his son.

When we got to San Francisco, the miners kept bragging about him as the man who'd freed them. And anyone who had a quarrel with Father had a quarrel with them, too.

No one in his right mind picks a fight with a group of miners whose muscles have been toughened by years of wrestling coal from rock. I won't say Father was the most popular man in Chinatown, but we were safe enough. Who says ghosts can't come back to life?

We had planned to stay with Uncle Sean; but Father's new triumph with the strike reminded Chinatown of his other past victories. And even his enemies were willing to listen to his opinions. So we got a place of our own in Chinatown and once again he was busy interpreting, organizing, and trying to improve Chinatown—whether people wanted it or not.

White Deer wound up at Uncle Bright Star's, and some of Father's other classmates fled the troubles around the country and settled in San Francisco too. With Uncle Sean we had our own small group of friends whom we could trust with our lives.

* * *

Sometimes it gets a little scary in San Francisco because we have the same Western fools as back in Rock Springs, so it's worth your life to go into certain parts of the city. And sometimes they invade the Chinatown here and smash things and beat up any Chinese they can catch.

When they're not around, there are the Chinatown brotherhoods, and they're just as bad. They're fighting all the time to control the drugs and brothels. It seems like I hear gunshots almost every night. And you have to be ready to duck in the daytime, too.

Father, though, has rolled up his sleeves to change all that; and this time I'm going to help. For better or for worse, Chinatown's my home, and I'm here to stay.

This Christmas, Michael and his mother will be coming in to San Francisco. With Uncle Sean's help, we've found them work in a fancy mansion.

The first chance Michael and I get, I want us to sneak up to the roof some evening and look at the stars, and remember Star Rock and the sound of the vanished ocean. And I know we'll feel that same peace again.

And maybe that feeling will spread outward from us, through the streets, beyond the city, and over the world.

And the ugly ghosts will disappear just like they did from Michael's house; and they'll only be flowers dreaming beneath the stars.

AFTERWORD

Until the 1880s, there were two Chinese Americas: the urban one, which survives to this day, and a rural one, consisting of many small Chinatowns that dotted the western states. A series of pogroms and massacres—as happened in Rock Springs—wiped most of them out.

In 1882, despite the efforts of Chinese Americans, Congress passed the Chinese Exclusion Law, which was designed to halt most Chinese immigration and make it impossible for current residents to become citizens. That law created a set of hurdles for legitimate residents to bring their families from China, as I've tried to show in my earlier novel *Dragonwings*, in which a boy, Moon Shadow, tries to enter America.

Otter and his son, Joseph, are part of the fictional saga

the Golden Mountain Chronicles, about the Young family and their friends. The Purdys are also fictitious, though Mary Purdy is based on a "Grandma" Williams, who hid Chinese in her cellar. However, I cannot emphasize enough that Mary Purdy's character and past are fictitious and nothing like those of the heroic Mrs. Williams. Her actions, and those of others who hid Chinese that dreadful day, remind us that people of conscience can shine even in the grimmest times. If there is one key lesson to be learned from the Rock Springs massacre, it is that there is still hope for us all.

Though I have changed names of most of the participants, the incidents leading up to the massacre and the savagery itself are based on the accounts of both Chinese and American eyewitnesses—however, I have left out some of the more gruesome details. Nor would I try to invent the bloodthirsty Dr. Murray or the woman who danced upon the Chinese corpse. The laundrywomen were especially deadly with their revolvers. Miss Virginia, who turned away her Chinese students and then later looted their camp, is based upon the actions of a real minister's daughter.

Figures for the death toll vary; but at least twenty-five bodies were recovered for burial. Another twenty-six Chinese vanished in the wasteland; and the stories of the Chinese who survived there are horrific in themselves. It is said that Rock Springs had one of the highest death tolls of any American race riot. Officially there were fifteen wounded, but the real figures will never be known.

Though there were many witnesses, no one was ever convicted for the murders or the destruction. The grand jury was packed with sympathetic jurors, including Dr. Murray; and vigilante patrols allowed only their witnesses to testify.

The massacre of the Chinese "scab" miners in 1885 is in direct contrast to 1871, when Scandinavian miners were brought in to break a strike in the same coal mines. Whatever hard feelings were created did not end in murder.

Two historical notes: One of the American eyewitnesses says September 2, 1885, was a Chinese holiday; but I have been unable to find any corresponding holiday in the Chinese calendar. I also have been unable to find why Chinese and Americans went on working at one mine through the massacre.

Star Rock is imaginary; but otherwise I have tried to follow the geography of the area as best I could. Nor have I made up the disapproval that was leveled at illegitimate children in the nineteenth—and well into the twentieth—century.

I wish to express my gratitude to the many kind people who helped me with the research on this novel. First, a special word of thanks to Dr. Barbara Chatton, my fellow "banana slug" from the University of California at Santa

Cruz, who has been so extravagant with her time and help. As I wrote, I kept a fossilized shell (non–iron pyrite) that Ann Daniels, the Staff Archaeologist of Western Wyoming Community College, sent me along with many materials. Dr. Dudley Gardner from the same college was extremely kind in sharing his knowledge of the Chinese in Wyoming. I especially appreciate the attempts of Audra Oliver of the Rock Springs Historical Society, as well as those of Norma Jean Robins, a local historian, to answer my questions. Jean Brainerd, Reference Historian from the Wyoming State Archives, and Alan J. Ver Ploeg, Senior Staff Geologist of the Wyoming State Geological Survey, also sent reference matter.

If you are interested in further reading, here are some of the more useful books and articles that I consulted:

The Chinese Massacre at Rock Springs, Wyoming Territory, September 2, 1885. Boston: Franklin Press, 1886.

The History of the Union Pacific Coal Mines, 1868 to 1940. Omaha, Nebraska: The Colonial Press, 1940.

"Memorial of Chinese Laborers Resident at Rock Springs, Wyoming Territory, to the Chinese Consul of New York (1885)," in Cheng-Tsu Wu, ed., *"Chink!": A Documentary History of Anti-Chinese Prejudice in America* (New York: Meridian World Publishing, 1972), pages 152–166.

Rhode, Robert B. *Booms & Busts on Bitter Creek: A History of Rock Springs, Wyoming.* Boulder, Colorado: Pruett Publishing, 1987; reprint 1999.

Storti, Craig. *Incident at Bitter Creek: The Story of the Rock Springs Chinese Massacre.* Ames, Iowa: Iowa State University Press, 1991.

Wilde, Gisela. Transcript of written memoir from the Rock Springs Historical Society, 1982, page 6.

THE GOLDEN MOUNTAIN CHRONICLES

The Chinatown that I knew as a child was a small place where everyone knew one another—not just in the present time but in some cases extending back across the generations 150 years to the first gold miners. The Chinatown in my imagination is the same way: It's just as small, and all my characters also know one another across seven generations in the nine novels of the Golden Mountain Chronicles.

The Chinatown of my books grew out of two newspaper articles that I read about Fung Joe Guey, who built and flew his own airplane in 1909. I could see the scene of that flight, and so I put it down on paper; but then I had to explain why and how he had built the airplane in the first place. And so I like to tell readers that I wrote *Dragonwings* in reverse. I first wrote the ending, about an early Chinese

American aviator, Windrider, and his son, Moon Shadow, and then all the chapters that went in front of it.

However, almost immediately the characters introduced me to friends of theirs, like Bright Star, who told me about his adventures when he was a young man working on the Transcontinental Railroad in 1867. During the worst winter of the century, the Chinese had to live and labor beneath the snow. So at about the same time that I was writing down the scene of Windrider flying in his airplane, I also wrote a scene in which a young Chinese boy, Otter Young, walks through tunnels of snow to his buried cabin. But it took longer to research and write the rest of Otter's story, and it was twenty years before *Dragon's Gate* was ready to be published.

In between the writing of *Dragonwings* and *Dragon's Gate*, and then afterward, the characters kept insisting I meet other friends and family of theirs; and I couldn't refuse them any more than I could my grandmother or my Chinatown uncles and aunts when they wanted me to do something. I found that Windrider's and Otter's friends were just as fascinating, and I wound up writing their stories as well, until they wound up covering the adventures of seven Chinese American generations over 150 years of American history in the Golden Mountain Chronicles.

In *The Serpent's Children* and *Mountain Light*, Otter's uncle, Foxfire, told me about the desperate situation in southern

China that forced the first generation of Chinese to risk the deadly trip to California for the Gold Rush in 1849. As guests of the Golden Mountain—which is what they called America—they began their love affair with their new home, for the Golden Mountain was a source not only of wealth but also of new, striking ideas.

Because of their sacrifices, the next generation was raised in comfort in China, so the harsh life of the Golden Mountain was a rude shock to men like Otter, Foxfire's nephew in *Dragon's Gate*. And yet despite the dangers, Otter and others of his generation forged new bonds with America, and the challenges of living here only deepened their love for this country. For them, America became the legendary dragon's gate that allowed brave fish to become dragons.

In *The Traitor*, Joseph, Otter's son, was the first generation to be born in America, and he had to deal with prejudices not only from Americans but from some of the old-time Chinese Americans. The lonely Joseph struck up a friendship with a fellow outcast, white Michael Purdy, who was ostracized by the white Americans in their town. Their friendship became crucial to each other's survival when, in 1885, the Wyoming Territory exploded in one of the worst race riots in American history.

Yet the land of the Golden Mountain meant more than money and innovations; it was also a place to capture special dreams—as represented by the airplane in

Dragonwings. Against the backdrop of the Chinatown at the turn of the century, the pioneer aviator Windrider had a dream that he was once a dragon. To recapture the feeling of flight he experienced in his dream, he and his son, Moon Shadow, built a flying machine. At the same time, they were also involved in a kind of quest for that special moment when they could reaffirm the power of the imagination: that ability, which lies sleeping in each of us, to grasp with the mind what we cannot grasp with the hand. And they went on seeking that dream despite riots, earthquakes, and personal tragedy.

By the 1930s, Joseph's grandson, Barney, and his close friend, Calvin Chin, told me about the kinds of lives they led behind the invisible barriers that prejudice had raised around Chinatown. Within those walls, they led lives similar to those of white teenagers. In my forthcoming book *Red Warrior*, Barney and Calvin told me how they broke out of the ghetto to explore America as members of a professional basketball team. As celebrities, they were able to visit places that had driven out earlier generations of Chinese Americans. The story is based on a real Chinese American basketball team, the Hong Wah Kues, who barnstormed their way across America in the 1930s and even played the Harlem Globetrotters.

By the 1960s, however, the next generation—including Barney's daughter, Casey, and Calvin Chin's son, Craig—had become cut off from its original Chinese roots. When